Leader o

I only sing after lunch. Hey, I'm not being difficult, but I am the centerpiece, the linchpin, the . . . okay, I'll say it, I'm the star. I didn't ask for it, didn't demand it, but everybody knows that if an act is going to make it, there has to be a certain force at the center of it. The guy with the lips in the Rolling Stones. Kurt Cobain when he was still alive with Nirvana. The blond guy who tames tigers in the circus. Tom Jones.

Moi.

#3

SCRATCH AND THE SNIFFS

Also by Chris Lynch

THE HE-MAN WOMEN HATERS CLUB

#3

SCRATCH AND THE SNIFFS

Chris Lynch

HarperTrophy®
A Division of HarperCollinsPublishers

Scratch and the Sniffs
Copyright © 1997 by Chris Lynch
All rights reserved. No part of this book may be used or reproduced in any
manner whatsoever without written permission except in the case of brief
quotations embodied in critical articles and reviews. Printed in the United
States of America. For information address HarperCollins Children's
Books, a division of HarperCollins Publishers,
10 East 53rd Street, New York, NY 10022.

Library of Congress Cataloging-in-Publication Data
Lynch, Chris.
Scratch and the Sniffs / Chris Lynch.
   p.   cm. — (The He-Man Women Haters Club ; #3)
   Summary: Relates the humorous attempts of wheelchair-bound
Wolfgang to organize the members of the He-Man Women Haters Club
into a rock band.
ISBN 0-06-027416-6 (lib. bdg.). — ISBN 0-06-440657-1 (pbk.)
   [1. Bands (Music)—Fiction. 2 Clubs—Fiction. 3. Physically
handicapped—Fiction. 4. Humorous stories.] I. Title. II. Series:
Lynch, Chris.   He-Man Women Haters Club ; #3.
PZ7.L979739Sc   1997
[Fic]—dc21   96-47437
                                                                CIP
                                                                 AC

1   2   3   4   5   6   7   8   9   10
❖
First Edition

Contents

1
A Box of Chocolates

Hate is such a strong word.

I love it.

Because at least it says something. I figure, if you're going to open your mouth, you might as well say something. Who cares if we don't actually hate women—maybe we do, maybe we don't. It's how it sounds that counts. And the He-Man Women Haters Club sounds a lot tougher than the He-Man Couldn't-Get-a-Date-if-We-Wanted-to Club.

That's not me, of course, but it does cover most of the guys in my club.

That's right, *my* club. They've been wanting me to take control since the day I showed up, but I kept telling them, listen, you guys just aren't ready for the big leagues yet. But they just kept begging and begging, and then their first leader, Steven, belly flopped, and then the second, Jerome,

1

burrowed into his own belly button when the going got tough, and so the president of the United States called me himself and pleaded that I take over the situation. . . .

So I'll do it temporarily, until this ship is afloat again. Then they're on their own, 'cause I've got bigger things on my plate than wasting my time being president of everything.

The first thing they are going to notice about my leadership style is that I get to the point. These guys want to be He-Men, then all they have to do is listen up, and they'll learn what's what, and what isn't. I call 'em like I see 'em.

Forrest Gump, for instance. What's all this about life's a box of chocolates, you never know what you're gonna get? What kind of garbanzo is that? You take your finger and poke it up through the bottom of every chocolate, and then you know exactly what you're gonna get, right? So you can put back the lousy coconut and pick out the caramel cream you were after in the first place.

So why doesn't somebody make a movie out of me and *my* homespun philosophy and pay me sixty bazillion dollars and spin off impossibly handsome Wolfgang dolls and *Cookin' with the Wolf* cookbooks?

When I'm done, they will.

Now I really will get to the point. You'd like that, wouldn't you?

My name, in case you missed it, is Wolfgang. That's all you need to know about me, but I'm going to tell you more because I know what you're after. Because, as everybody knows, what is really important is how a person looks. I look like a kid in a wheelchair. You got something to say about that?

Didn't think so.

Swell. So let's talk about how the rest of them look.

Steven is, I suppose, in a way, in a very common way, what someone might describe as handsome. He's taller than me even when he's sitting, he has a swimmer's body, and sometimes it seems that girls actually like him. He has exactly thirty-nine chest hairs on him, which he'll be happy to tell you about, and I think he may have names for them all by now. There is a girl named Monica, who has a thing for Steven, and we can assume Steven has a thing for Monica, since every time she appears he makes a total butt of himself. The situation would be pretty darn funny to anyone who was inclined to be cruel and ridicule Steven from time to time.

3

Which would be me.

Steven claims to hate Monica. Steven doesn't deserve Monica.

I do.

The best thing about Steven is that he owns a very cool 1956 Lincoln that lives in his uncle's garage and is our official club headquarters. Steven doesn't deserve that car.

I do.

Then there's Jerome. You could carry Jerome around in your knapsack for a whole day if you wanted to, and you wouldn't even get a stiff back. But he's also a real brain box, and you know how they are. So you have to watch him every second. Jerome has this dream of being exactly like Steven. Please, don't ask me, all right? Unless it's the chest hair thing, I can't figure it out either.

Ling-Ling.

Ling-Ling. Any description of He-Man Ling is going to sell him short. He's a giant, like twelve feet tall and nine hundred pounds. He reads comic books one hundred percent of the time and when he's done with one, he eats it like a government secret. He's so pale that if he was naked—

Oh my god!

Sorry. If he was, naked, and standing against a

4

white wall, you couldn't see him. Couldn't see the wall, either, for that matter. He has an excellent collection of big-head hats, we got him out of an on-line computer advertisement, and he hardly ever says anything unless you ask him to. He's like Arnold Schwarzenegger, if Arnold was just a little tougher. The club really does revolve around Ling-Ling. Never mind that, the country, the whole world, revolves around Ling-Ling.

He's actually a big fat spaz who cries all the time, but I like to say nice things about him.

So as you can see, the first order of business under the new regime is clear.

Recruitment.

2
Scratch

He was hanging at the entrance to the subway when I passed by on the way to the club. If getting attention was the real point for street performers no matter what their particular act was, this guy was one successful busker.

"You stink, man," a hippie screamed at him. You really have to work to get a hippie to scream you stink man.

"Thanks," the kid said, without even looking up from the fretboard of his yellow guitar.

The color of the guitar matched his long stringy hair. He had no shirt on, exposing a set of ribs so jagged you could climb them like little stairs. His cheeks looked like he was sucking them in on purpose, and he had hand-drawn pictures of snakes and skeletons—he didn't have to look far for a model—inked all over his upper body. I could tell he did the artwork himself, because most of it was upside down.

"You don't stink," I said. I meant it. He was grinding away on that guitar, feeding it through a mini amplifier at his feet, but getting huge sound out of it. I didn't recognize any of the songs he played—didn't even know if they were songs—but I loved the *amount* of stuff he was getting out of it. It sounded like when the trash truck goes into mash mode and there's a filing cabinet inside.

"I know I don't. But thanks anyway, man." He looked up when he said it, flipping his head left and right like a horse to get the hair off his face. That exposed the most awesome part of the look yet. Starting at his left temple and zigging its way diagonally across and down to his right ear was the most vivid zipper scar I had ever seen.

"Wicked scar," I said, nodding and wheeling up closer to admire it. "No kidding, truly excellent."

The kid played on. "That's no scar. That's a scratch."

"Ya? Well, I bet Frankenstein'd be jealous."

"Pshhh," he said, waving me off. He stopped playing to pull up the leg of his hugely baggy, filthy dungarees. "This, is a scar," he said, pointing to a spiraling fat purple gouge that ran up the entire outside of his leg and spread an inch wide.

I nodded again. "You're right, that's a scar. What'd they sew you up with, baseball glove rawhide stitch?"

"What, they? Did it myself."

He went back to playing. Then I noticed he was missing half of the middle finger on his right hand.

"How'd you lose that?" I said, pointing rudely.

"Bit it off during a math test. How'd you lose those?" he shot back, pointing at my rubber legs.

"Didn't," I said. "I'm just lazy."

He smiled broadly. His teeth too were that same banana color as the guitar and hair.

"You got a name?" I asked.

"No," he answered.

"I'm Wolf."

"Scratch," he said.

"Huh?"

"I said Scratch."

How did he know I was itchy? It was uncanny. I started clawing at myself, just under the . . .

"No, I mean, that's my name. That's what you can call me, Scratch."

"Oh." Too bad. I was working up such a good scratching for myself, my foot was about to start thumping. "So how come you're out here?"

"Making a living."

I looked into the top hat on the ground in front of him. "Not much, you're not."

In response, Scratch turned up his volume to the max and started grinding on his instrument, aiming it at me like a machine gun to try and blast me away. It was way beyond what the speaker could handle, and it sounded now like two trains colliding over and over down in the subway.

"Listen to that," I hollered. "You're a genius. You shouldn't be wasting your time here."

"You got a better idea for how I should be wasting my time?"

"Of course I have a better idea," I said, rolling up close and patting my new man on the back. "An outstanding idea. You pack up and come with me, and you'll see, I have *all* the best ideas."

This was the situation when we got to the club: Ling was inside the Lincoln, in the backseat, reading comics. Jerome was walking speedy circles around the car, muttering about something, worrying himself bald about something. Lars, Steven's uncle, who owns the garage we club in and so we have to be at least a little nice to him, was leaning in the back window of the car, rambling on and on in Ling's ear about something big. Always something big with Lars, always something he knew everything about. Ling was not listening to Lars.

And nobody was listening to Jerome. This was the situation when we arrived.

This was always the situation when I arrived.

Except usually Steven was already there. This time, he came in right behind me, hauling a new recruit just like I was.

"Hey," Steven called from behind.

Scratch and I stopped and turned around.

"What's this?" he asked, pointing to Scratch.

"New blood," I said, slapping my man on his bare pink back. "What do you have there?" I asked in return. I don't think it bothered either of us much to be there talking about two fellow humans as if they were new socket wrenches. The new guys didn't seem to mind either. It's a guy thing.

Steven pulled up alongside his. "Meet The Killer. He's our newest club member—once we vote him in, of course. Tell Wolfgang why they call you Killer," Steven said proudly. "Go ahead, tell him why they call you that."

Could have been for his looks alone, I thought. And I don't mean handsome, lady-killer-type killer looks. I mean everybody-killer looks. The kid was just as tall as Ling, and just as skinny as Scratch. He looked like Abe Lincoln, with all the sharp-cut face bones, black curly hair, and limbs that stretched on forever in every direction. But he was a lot more *Jurassic Park* than Honest Abe, with a bottom jaw that stuck out about an inch farther than the top, and eye sockets so deep there was no way of telling what color was in there. Score one for Steven already: He had found his recruit under a bigger rock than I'd found mine under.

The Killer smiled proudly. "Shoot, I don't like braggin'," he said.

Which was when I realized he was a big bag o' nothin'. *Everybody* likes to brag.

"Oh, go on," I prodded. "Brag."

"Well then, it has to do with when I was a kid in Muscle Shoals, Alabama. There was just me and this big ol' crazy alligator and all I had was a rock—"

"Nice story there, Killer," I said, and spun toward the back of the garage, pulling Scratch along with me.

"Hey," Steven called, chasing after us. "You didn't even let him finish his story."

"What?" I asked, but I kept on going. "What? I thought that was the end. You mean there's more to the story?"

"Sure," Killer said.

"Oh," I said. "I didn't *realize*."

Killer got himself all pumped up again. I love to see a guy get pumped up.

11

"Let me guess," I said. "Ahhhh, you . . . *killed* the alligator."

You could hear some of the air hiss out of him. "Well, um, yes sir, I did indeed."

"Wait, wait. You killed him . . ." I closed my eyes and put my fingers to my temples like those old crapola fortune-tellers. "You killed him . . . with the *rock*, am I right?"

The Killer got all red, staring down at me. Then he turned on Steven. "You *told* him already," he snapped, thumping Steven in the chest with his big country-boy fist.

"Hey, Steven," I said. "I really like your new boy. Good thing there's no written exam to get into this club, huh?"

Steven huffed.

"That mean I'm in?" Killer asked, rejuvenated.

I shrugged. "Well, hold on there, pardner. I do have an oral exam first."

He squinted at me.

"Oral. It has to do with your mouth. You have to speak."

"I can do that," he said. Then he looked to Steven, to back him up, I guess. Steven had his eyes covered.

"Okay, ready, Tex?"

"Alabama."

"Ready? The question is: Are you a dink?"

The squint got so tight he looked in pain. He turned to his man Steven, who was already sorry he'd gotten into this. "Just answer him, for crying out loud," Steven snapped.

"No. I am not now, nor have I ever been, a dink."

"Fine, you're in."

I quickly turned and wheeled myself over to the Lincoln, where Jerome and Ling were watching with great interest. They looked a little nervous at the new presences in the club.

"Guys, I want you to meet the two newest members of the He-Man Women Haters Club. This is Scratch, and this is Huckleberry."

"Nah, that's 'Killer,'" he said nicely, as if I had made an honest mistake. "Not Huckleberry. Y'all can call me Killer. But what is it with that Huckleberry name, anyway? Is there somebody by that name who looks like me or somethin'? I hear it all the time lately."

I got closer to Steven. "I want to thank you, Steve-o. I'm going to love having him around. What is he, like, a birthday present for me or something?"

13

"Wait a minute," Jerome squawked. "That's not the way this works. We all have to vote before any new—"

"Ling," I said. "You got any problem with our two new members? Do they have your vote?"

"Okay," Ling said, with his patented one-shoulder shrug.

"Well then, Jerome," I said. "The candidates both have the votes of He-Man Wolf, and He-Man Steven, since we each voted for the other's nominee—right, Stevie?" Steven had by now slithered into the backseat of the car, hidden his face in *The Fantastic Four*, and merely grunted when I needed him to. "And since He-Man Ling-Ling has also thrown his weight—sorry, Ling—behind them, the guys now have at least three votes out of the original He-Man Four. So they're already in. You can still vote no, as a protest or something, but would you really want to do that and then have to see them all the time? We could do a secret ballot, of course, but I think, once they see the tally is three to one, and they do the math—"

"Whoa," Killer said. "Nobody told me about no math bein' involved in all this. . . ."

"Okay, *one* of them might be able to figure out who blackballed them."

Good old Jerome. He's a lot of things, but he is not unreasonable. He walked up to the new guys and shook their hands. "Nice to meet you, Mr. Scratch. Look forward to working with you, Mr. Killer."

God, I'm great at this power-wielding thing, and I didn't even know it.

And it feels so goooood.

It's like discovering chocolate all over again.

3
Cecil and the Moose Musk

"Okay, so what I want to know is, what does your guy bring to the club? Huh, Wolf?" This was Steven talking. "I mean, we know what The Killer brings. I picked him carefully, recruited him hard. Every club in town was trying to get this guy, and who wouldn't? Look at him . . . *The Killer!*"

So I looked at him.

"What's your real name, Killer?" I asked.

"For real?"

Sigh. "Yes, your real name for real."

"Cecil."

"Cecil, that wasn't really an alligator you killed all by yourself with that rock, now, was it?"

Cecil shook his head. "It was a frog."

"There now, don't you feel better telling the truth?"

"It was a mighty big frog, though. That's a fact."

"I don't doubt it. And I'm sure you done slayed him right good."

"Well, truth? Truth is he wasn't completely *not* dead in the first place, when I hit him."

"Wasn't completely *not* . . . ? Cecil, you hit an already dead frog with a rock in Muscle Shoals, Alabama. Then you brought that story all the way up here, and named yourself The Killer based on the heroics of that very tale. Have I got that right?"

"Guess I never fully assembled all the parts of the story together like that before. But, yes."

"If it's okay with you, I think I'll call you Cecil."

"Sure. Okay if I still call myself The Killer?"

"Knock yourself out."

I grabbed his hand just in time.

"It's just an expression, Cecil. Just an expression."

By the end of this conversation, Steven had already retreated to the underside of the Lincoln. I wheeled myself over to where his legs were sticking out. I could tell from the stillness of him that he wasn't actually working on anything, just lying there. It's the traditional He-Man refuge. Just ask your dad, he'll tell you.

"So let me show you what *my* guy contributes to the organization," I said to the feet. "Yo, Scratch, fire it up, will ya?"

Scratch then unzipped his guitar from its soft case, unstrapped the portable amp from his back, and plugged in. As soon as he started his loud tuning up—which sounded awesome, like he was sawing a cat in half—he had everybody's attention. Ling lifted himself out of the back of the car, and Steven slid himself out from under it. Jerome and Cecil, who had begun explaining to each other what life was like on their respective home planets, broke off talks to come and listen. Lars bolted for his office.

"Oh my god," Jerome said. "What is that?"

"Music, ya fool," I said.

"That's not music," he shot back. "It sounds like dentist's tools."

"Shows you what you know. My boy's a genius."

"No, I'm not," Scratch said, then turned the volume way up high.

"Ouch," Jerome whined. "It *feels* like dentist's tools. Somebody give me Novocain."

I balled up a fist and waved it at him. "I'll give you Novocain."

Steven was into it, staring at Scratch as he worked. He looked like a real guitar god, his wiry, ink-stained body bent over almost in half, his golden hair hanging way down over his face.

"Hey, he's really good," Steven said.

Scratch nudged his volume up again, then slashed hard across the strings.

"Hey," Cecil said excitedly. "Are we a band, too? This is so great. Is there a washboard around someplace? I gotta join in."

I think we were all about to jump on that when we were stopped short by Lars, who came streaking down from his office, headed straight for our new He-Man guitar man.

Party's over, I figured.

"Genius," Lars yelped, rushing right up to Scratch.

This worried me deeply, Lars and me thinking the same thing.

Scratch didn't even look at him. He just played harder, faster, louder.

"You're a punk!" Lars screamed. "Kid, you're a real live punk!"

The Killer jumped between them, standing right up in Lars's face. "You want me to bop this guy, Scratch?" he asked.

"What's a punk?" the punk himself asked. I couldn't tell if he was just toying with Lars. Lars makes you want to toy with him.

"What's a punk? Come on. I can tell by the way

you play, you know all about them. You know, the Ramones, the Stooges, the Pistols. I *know* you know Johnny Rotten."

"We know Johnny Chesthair," Jerome cracked.

"Do you know Johnny *Shut-up*?" Steven cracked back.

Now, *this* was fun. Maybe it was punk, maybe it wasn't, but I certainly liked the atmosphere around the club now. This was the style I wanted for my regime.

"Well, as a matter of fact, Lars," I said, "we are starting a band."

All together, like one dopey choir, my boys all said, "Huunnhh?"

"See?" I told Lars. "We already do harmonies."

"I was in a band once," Lars said. "We called ourselves the Blood Blisters, and I could show you kids a thing or two about—"

"You guys play music?" Scratch asked.

"Of course we do," I said.

"We do?" Jerome asked.

"We do," I reassured him.

"No," he said back. "I don't think we do."

"What do you play?" Steven asked me.

The problem I had here was, my guys had no imagination. They took everything so literally.

"I, you know, play this and that."

"So tell us, what's *this*?"

You're really starting to bug me there, Steve-o. "I'm the *manager*, okay?"

He smiled. "And what is *that*?"

Grrrrr. "I . . . sing," I muttered, to my own great surprise.

Well, if nothing else, I had managed to bring more humor to the club than our two previous leaders combined. Coincidentally, they were the very two who were now laughing so hard I looked around the garage floor for a stray tonsil or two.

"I said something funny?" I asked coolly.

"Anyway, we were the hottest band in town for a while, no kidding . . ." Lars plowed on.

"I want to play the drums," Ling blurted.

Everybody stopped. We turned our attention to Ling-Ling.

"Ever played the drums before?" I asked.

"No," he said.

We waited.

"But I know where I can get some. My grandfather used to play in a silent movie theater band."

"You're hired," Scratch said.

"What, are you joking?" I asked Scratch. "Just like that? Is that how you select instrumentalists?"

He shrugged. "That's how all bands do it. Whoever has a drum kit is the drummer."

"I wanted to play drums," Steven said.

"I wanted to play drums," Jerome said.

"Tough," I said. "You can't all be—"

"Why not?" Scratch said. "Ling, is it a big drum kit? Could you share?"

Ling nodded. "But I want to play that big giant drum myself."

"Oh, this is stupid. One guitar and three drummers . . ."

"Don't forget my washboard," Cecil said.

"Oh no, we wouldn't forget. . . ."

"And of course," Lars added, "I have my own—"

"Get outta here, you," I barked. "Go fix a car or something."

Scratch was laughing now, for the first time since I met him. "This is gonna be fun," he said.

"If you say so," I said. Then I rolled up close to whisper to him. "All kidding aside, Scratch, you will teach us, right? So we don't make butts of ourselves."

"Teach you what?"

"You know, teach us to play."

He laughed some more, his mouth opening all the way to show that just about half of his teeth were missing. "I don't know how to *play*," he said. "That was just screechy-noise I was doing before."

I deflated.

"Don't worry," he said, putting a hand on my shoulder. "It doesn't matter anyway. Knowing how just gets in the way."

I wished I'd said that.

"What'll we call ourselves? That's the most important thing," Steven said.

"Well, I figure we should try 'The Wolf Gang,' " *one* of us offered. "It's got kind of a ring to it."

"Kind of a *gong* to it, you mean," Steven replied.

Scratch just shook his head. "You don't name a band after the manager. You name it after the guitar player. Everybody knows that."

Scratch. Scratch?

"No," I said.

He quietly started packing up his stuff.

"Okay," I said. "But 'Scratch' sounds like it's just you. We need to be 'Scratch' and the . . . Somethings."

Once again, as in all our times of need, Ling-Ling stepped up to the plate.

"I got this card," he said, holding the card up in the air and examining it. "It fell out of my *American Survivor* magazine. It's an ad for a deodorant for hunters called Moose Musk. See, what you do is you scratch this little circle right here—"

"Yesss!" I said, and Steven seconded it.

"Yeeee-haw," Cecil yelled. "I love it too. Scratch and the Moose Musk."

Jerome jumped up. "I can't take much more of this," he squealed. He walked right up to The Killer—who was about three Jeromes tall—and started poking him in the belly with his sharp little index finger. "Scratch and the Sniffs, Huckleberry! They want to call us Scratch and the Sniffs!"

Jerome was still poking the stunned Killer as I rolled it around. Scratch and the Sniffs.

"I like it," I said, making it official. "It's pungent."

4
The Rest Is History

Day one of the great musical venture. I arrived at the door to Lars's garage to find He-Man Cecil sitting there on the sidewalk strumming—no, he was not kidding—his washboard.

Chikka-ching, chikka-ching, chikka-chikka-chikka-ching.

At first, I couldn't even speak. And we all know how unusual *that* is.

I hovered over him as he played, his long legs spread out across almost the whole sidewalk from the base of Lars's cinderblock building to the curb. He looked up at me with a simple, pleased smile, as if I would find all this entertaining.

"Don't you ever get embarrassed about anything?" I asked him.

"Not most days, no," he answered cheerfully.

Then I noticed the big brown jug at his side. "Ah," I said, pointing at it. "This explains a lot. You're a drinker. Now it makes sense."

Cecil laughed. "That ain't for drinkin', that's for playin'." He put down the washboard—good—and picked up the jug—less good.

Ooom-pah, Ooom-pah, Ooom-pah, Ooom-pah, Ooom-ooom-pah-pah-pah.

"Stop that," I ordered. "That's enough now. Get all this stuff inside before people notice us."

People had already noticed. A man in a business suit stuffed a dollar into the mouth of the jug on his way by.

"Don't encourage him," I said to the man.

"Thank you, sir," Cecil chirped, then gave the jug a shake. It jingled.

I peeked into the jug. There was a blanket of silver and green at the bottom.

"You made all that this morning?" I asked.

"I gotta tell you," Cecil said. "I thought Muscle Shoals was nice, but this is the *friendliest* town I ever been to. And do they ever appreciate the arts."

"Scratch probably wouldn't make that much in a year," I said, more to myself and to the gods of glorious money than to Cecil. My manager muscles were twitching like mad.

"Let's get inside, Jug-head, we got practicing and tour-planning to do."

"I don't think I partic'ly care for that *Jug-head* term."

"Oh no, it's a compliment. It means your brain is too big for any normal-size head. . . ."

Scratch was already there, practicing his chops.

"This is good," I said. "I like this. As manager, I have to say I'm very impressed with your work habits, Mr. Scratch. Brand-new to the He-Man Women Haters, and already you're arriving to meetings before anyone else."

"Ya, well . . ." Scratch said sheepishly.

"Ya, well . . . go on, why don't you tell him?" Lars said, a little agitated.

"Tell me what?" I wanted to know.

"Tell you the reason I'm here first, he means. The reason I'm here first today is because I was here last yesterday."

"And all the time in between," Lars added.

"Oh," I said. "I see."

"What?" asked Cecil, bringing up the rear of the conversation. "Did you forget to go home?"

I just looked at Cecil. That's all you can do with him, really.

"What home?" Scratch mumbled.

Everyone was quiet then. What do you say to something like that?

Lars came up with something. "Ya, well, the rotten punk ate a whole can of Pringles and a tub of peanut butter out of my office."

Cecil whispered in my ear. "Now, *rotten punk,* is that a good—?"

I shook my head. "No, it's the other kind." Then I turned back to Scratch. "You don't have anyplace else?"

The slamming of the door broke things up for the moment as Steven and Jerome came in.

"Nephew, we need to discuss your new boy here," Lars said, pointing at Scratch.

Steven walked the length of the garage, approached the group, passed the group, and went right to his car. "That one's not mine," he said, sitting behind the wheel of the Lincoln.

I turned to start up with Lars, but Steven interrupted things again.

"Hey!" he yelled. "Where's my steering wheel cover?" He bounded up out of the car. "The original, leather steering wheel cover that felt so soft and nice in my hands. Where is it?"

"He *ate* it," Lars said, again pointing to our guitar player.

We all turned to Scratch now.

"That can't be true," I said.

Steven stalked toward Scratch, who started backing up. "That was a forty-year-old piece of leather," he growled.

"I guess that's why it was so tender," Scratch said.

That was *it*, of course. Steven threw himself at the much bigger Scratch, but I guess Scratch was one of those lover-not-a-fighter types, because all he did was cover up. I laid rubber wheeling myself between the two of them, and when I got there we discovered the real heart of the matter.

". . . show *you* who's boss . . ." Steven snarled as he locked his hands on my shoulders and tried to wrestle me down.

I suppose it was only right that Steven and I should do a little brawling for the new guys. We shouldn't have any secrets in the HMWHC.

"Okay then, Mr. Chesthair," I said, and grabbed him by his shoulders. He pulled, I pushed, and the two of us rolled from the wheelchair onto the greasy garage floor.

"Oh my god," Cecil said. "He's attacking a crippled person. I never seen nobody do nothin' like that before in my whole entire life."

"No?" Jerome said in a bored voice. "Stick around, you'll see it here all the time."

I was trying to get my famous death grip on Steven, but it was a lot of work: the sneaky sonofagun, he'd been working out behind my back. His arms, his chest, his back, they all felt bulkier than last time I laid a beating on him.

Bang! He got a hand loose and slapped me straight in the forehead. So I took a fist and clubbed him in the chest.

I love that gasping sound he makes when I do that.

But really, I found that it wasn't as much fun as it should have been. Because, well, he was right. He was already feeling bad because I was in charge of the club that used to be his, and then I brought in a guy who was eating parts off his car.

I felt bad for him.

Whoa. Who said that?

I owed him something.

"Ouch," I said when he got me in a headlock that really didn't hurt that much. Then he squeezed tighter, rolled me over, and pinned me to the floor.

"There," he said, and gave me one last little shove as he got up off me. As I lay very flat on the floor, ten feet away from my chair, Steven started walking toward his seat in the car—the place he usually goes to decompress—when suddenly he stopped, turned, and stared at me.

I was cool. Started humming, stared at the ceiling, tapped my fingers on the filthy floor.

He came over with my chair, offered me both hands, and helped me back up into it.

Not that I really needed any help.

When the dust had settled, Steven and I were hardly even an issue anymore. Cecil had already picked up on the club trick of ducking under the Lincoln for escape. Jerome was over in one corner helping Ling-Ling with the entire percussion section he'd carried in on his back. Scratch was off in another corner trying to fend off Lars.

"So we'll call it a wash," Lars said. "You don't have to pay me anything for the Pringles, and you let me play with your band."

"Ummm, I really don't know . . ." Scratch said.

I hurried to his rescue. "What's the matter with you, Lars? All your own friends off at summer camp or something? Go play someplace else."

"All right then," Lars snapped. "I'll go play someplace else. But so will he. No more living in the garage."

Scratch shrugged. He really didn't seem to care one way or the other.

"Wait," I said as Lars stormed away. I looked at Scratch, who was plucking quietly at his strings. I felt sorry for him.

That was *twice* I felt sorry. In one day!

I knew I was going to hate myself in the morning.

"What do you play, Lars?" I asked in a whispery, cautious voice.

He was psyched, much more excited really than a person his age should get. "Guitar, of course. Just like him. Only better, because I'm a pro."

Hated myself already, well ahead of schedule.

"Well, Lars, maybe we could let you just sit in with us, once in a while, after we hear you play."

"Yeeee-hoooo!" he said, jumping up and kicking his heels together like the green moron on the Lucky Charms commercials. "I'll bring my axe tomorrow," he said as he skipped off to his office.

"You do that," I said. "You bring your axe, and I'll bring *mine*."

Scratch and I looked at each other and sighed. "How bad could it be, right?" he offered.

I shivered.

The six actual members of the club—the deep six—gathered around Ling's grandfather's big old drum kit. Ling, Jerome, and Steven, our drum team, were already negotiating their parts.

"But why?" Jerome moaned. "Why, why, why am I always stuck with these jerky, demeaning jobs?"

"There is nothing wrong with being the per-cussionist," Steven said as he clutched the snare and tom-tom with what was left of his might. Ling-Ling had already made it clear to everyone that he was claiming the family right to his grandpap's bass drum. Ling was happy. Steven had then carved out his territory with the other two drums. Which left Jerome with . . . the other stuff.

"I quit," Jerome huffed.

"It's no reason to quit," I said. It probably didn't help that I was laughing at him while I said it.

"See, Wolf knows. Only the geeks get to play this stuff."

"Hey, there have been some *hot* tambourine players in music history," Steven said.

"Shut up," Jerome said.

"No, really, the Beach Boys have one, I think." Now Scratch started laughing.

"And I saw some at the airport in Atlanta when I flew up from Muscle Shoals," said a very helpful Cecil.

"I mean it," Jerome said, his little head throwing off steam in the July heat. "I'm really going to quit over this one."

"And there was that little girl in the Partridge Family," Lars called from way off. "She was a dynamite tambourinist."

"Right," Jerome said. "And what else do I have here? *Triangle*. I get to play the stupid triangle! What do you think, that I don't know what this means? Playing triangle makes you like king of all the dweebs. Look at school bands—which are filled with geeks to begin with, right?—even in the school band, the lowliest lame-o of them all gets assigned to ping the triangle. Even guys in *band* beat up on the triangle player, and that is as low as it gets."

This was getting to be a first-rate performance. Jerome had jumped up onto the roof of the Lincoln to scream his case, and if he could muster up this much mustard all the time, we might have to make him the group's front man.

"I'm not going to take it anymore," he railed. "Look, Ling and Steven didn't even leave me any sticks to play with. *They* each have a pair of drumsticks. What am I supposed to hit my *one* cymbal with, my face?"

I wheeled cautiously up to the car, laughing all the same. It was hard to even talk. "If we get you a pair of sticks, will you come down and join us?"

He stood up there hyperventilating. He thought it over.

"No. I want to trade with somebody. I don't care who, I just don't want to be the biggest dink in the act."

To the rescue came the ever-gallant Cecil, who silently offered Jerome his washboard.

"Fine," Jerome said, stomping down off the car. "I'll play the stupid triangle."

5
The Kinks

Maybe it was time to find out if we could play.

Scratch, whether he wanted to admit it or not, was great. Every morning when I showed up at the club, he was already there, churning out some nasty beautiful noise or another. But when the rest of us came along to take up our positions alongside him, well, that's where we had to work out some kinks.

The first problem was Lars. He just wouldn't go away. He became—when he was wearing his protective red Fender Stratocaster guitar and his favorite tight black muscle shirt—the guy you could not insult. Believe me, I tried.

"Hey, Lars," I said. "Nice shirt, but doesn't a person stop growing out of their clothes at some point?"

He strummed away, smiling. "Oh, I stopped growing when I was in eighth grade."

"No, I mean *physically*."

He just laughed and laughed, as if he had any idea what I had even said. The old crock, he was just having himself too good a time to be really bothered by my cracks.

We'd have to put a stop to *that*.

Two thirds of the drum team were all business. Steven and Jerome showed up to work early, took their places at the kit, and tippy-tapped around the instruments, trying to feel their way in. I gave everybody a lot of space those first few days, trying not to put too much pressure on, but I was listening closely. Steven, in particular, didn't sound half bad. From his setup halfway across the garage from the guitars, he would coolly try to lock on to whatever the guitarists were noodling with. When he had a beat on it, he'd slip himself in there with a *tap, ta ba-ba-bap,* using only one drum at a time so as not to get too complicated. He fit, and didn't get in the way at all. Good boy, Steven.

Jerome eventually warmed to his job, and in no time sounded like one of the top ten triangle players in the whole neighborhood. When his confidence built, he would move from that to the tambourine, to the cymbal, hitting each one once and only once, before moving on to the next instrument. *Ping . . .*

one-two-three . . . *ting* . . . one-two-three . . . You wouldn't call it percussion, so much as flavor, but it was . . . tidy.

You know the phrase *different drummer*?

The day we had scheduled for our first actual jam together, Ling-Ling treated it like it was his own personal opening night at Caesar's Palace.

He wore a purple silk bowling shirt with "Vic the Stick" embroidered over the pocket. He wore enormous Elton John 1970s pink sunglasses.

"*Sin*glasses, I call them," he said.

I couldn't let that one go. "Hah. What sin did you ever commit, *Lung*?" They can't stand it when I call them body parts. "Eat the last Fig Newton? Leave the toilet paper roller empty, you ol' desperado?"

Ling lowered his glasses and looked over them with a grim, dramatic squint. "You don't want to know what I did. Serious stuff, another life. It's best for you if you know nothing, in case they come around looking." He pushed his glasses back up his meaty face, adjusted his Robin Hood hat with the yellow and green feathers, and sat down with his big fat mystery life behind the bass drum.

"Hey, *Vic*," I said to him. "You're a mental case."

"Hey, who loves ya, Wolf-man?"

And I always thought it was the lead singer who was supposed to be a group's Hollywood prima donna nutball. Fortunately, we had a lead singer who had his head on straight.

"Now, what we want out of this is money, right? Is everybody clear on that?" I asked as we took our places for the first in-house test of our talent. "That's what music is all about, as everyone knows. You get people all excited and worked up and crazy until they want to give you their money. Then you politely take it from them. So we will have to not stink, first off. Then we have to be a little different, second off, which shouldn't be too much of a problem since we are the world's first punk-hillbilly-jug-drum-corps band."

"You got honest-to-god hillbillies in this band?" Cecil asked aggressively. He threw down his washboard and jumped up into a fighting stance. "Who is it?"

"Easy there, Tumbleweed. Just sit back down and chew off a hunk of tobacco to calm yourself."

He did. He pulled the sticky-looking chaw out of the bib of his overalls. "Aw, but it ain't even real plug, y'know. It's only a wedge of bubble gum that I soak overnight in a glass of Dr Pepper to make it look right. My maw says I can't be chewin' the real stuff till—"

Chwaaaannnggg.

The key, of course, to good guitar playing is timing.

"Nice timing, Scratch," I said, clapping and hooting him on. He went with it, turning up his volume, sawing on the strings, creating distortion, buzz, squeals and screams.

"Yeah!" I yelped into my microphone, which was actually plugged into an old stereo. "Yeah, baby, yeah!"

I have to be honest. I was kind of hoping my voice was going to sound a little better, a little stronger, a little more . . . musical when it came out of speakers than when it came out of my mouth. This was a disappointment. I yelled into it—no words yet, just attitude—harder and harder to make it sound better.

"Hey, Pavarotti," Steven yelled. "Maybe you should turn it *on.*"

Well, that was pretty embarrassing.

"Never mind me," I said. "You just play your drum, rhythm slave. Or do you need me to come over there and read you the directions?"

True, Steven was just more or less staring as

Scratch played. As was everybody. They couldn't make anything out of it.

"Ah, I don't know the song," Steven said.

"Ya," chimed the other players. The washboard, bass drum, and triangle remained unplayed.

Lars started to strum something that seemed distantly related to what Scratch was doing. Very distantly related, like a twelfth cousin or something.

Scratch was not concerned with our struggle. He did not slow down or speed up or simplify. He did not explain, and he did not instruct.

Ping.

"There!" I yelled. "See. See. Jerome's got it. Jerome knows. Way to go there, Jerome."

"It's a *triangle,* ya dope," Steven said to me. "That doesn't tell us anything. Jerome doesn't need to know what's going on. He can go *ping* to whatever Scratch plays."

"Hey," Jerome snapped, visibly wounded. "I'm working over here, I'll have you know. I am *trying* to make art out of this, and if you think it's so easy, you can just take this triangle and fit it—"

"All right already," Steven said. "I was only—"

"Ya, well, if you'd spend a little more time beating on your drum, and a little less beating on your hairy johnny chest, maybe we could work this out."

"Go Jerome," I laughed, which naturally incited Steven, who began slamming on his snare with both sticks and staring so hard at me that I thought he was going to launch himself right over the percussion section into my lap. We can all imagine what he was fantasizing he was beating on, can't we?

"I love this!" Lars squealed. "This is just like the Pistols! They hated each other's guts too."

"We hate each other?" Cecil asked. Poor Cecil. "I thought we was a club that liked each other but hated women."

"That's right," Jerome kicked in. "We do hate women. We don't hate each other."

Steven looked at me. "Oh yes we do," he said.

I had to laugh. Really loudly, through my microphone. This was finally starting to be fun.

But the truth was, Steven turned out to be the motor. As he tattooed his drum, everyone picked up on his savagery. Ling *boom-boomed*. Cecil *chikka-chikka'd* his washboard. Jerome murdered his poor tambourine. The way Steven absolutely attacked the two drums he had—still one at a time—inspired the rest of us to follow him. His arms extended fully as he beat the skin off the snare with a might I had never seen—not in his fighting anyway. It wasn't pretty, it wasn't coordinated, it wasn't particularly musical. But it was ferocious.

It was us.

"Hey, Steve-o," I taunted. "You got something personal against that particular drum, or you working on some kind of a therapy thing? You got a problem you want to share with the rest of the group?"

He just kept slamming away, staring at me—which was fine, if it got him playing.

"Yo, Wolfie," Jerome cut in. "We hear you talking, but, you know, at least we're contributing."

"Ya, wheel-daddy," the new jazz-version Ling added. "You talkin' a good game, but you ain't showin' nobody nothin'."

Ah. So the moment had arrived.

6
Time to Howl

I only sing after lunch. Hey, I'm not being difficult, but I am the centerpiece, the linchpin, the . . . okay, I'll say it, I'm the star. I didn't ask for it, didn't demand it, but everybody knows that if an act is going to make it, there has to be a certain force at the center of it. The guy with the lips in the Rolling Stones. Kurt Cobain when he was still alive with Nirvana. The blond guy who tames tigers in the circus. Tom Jones.

Moi.

I can't help it if I'm cursed with what we in the business call "star power." Charisma. No kidding, everywhere I go, people point at me on the street, they smile, they whisper, they gawk. I can't usually hear, but I can tell what they're saying. "You've got it, cowboy," is one probability, along with "That's a lot of man there."

So it is my responsibility—my *duty*, for crying

out loud—to preserve and nurture my gifts. That's why I can't strain my voice before lunchtime.

And also that gave me more time to figure out how the heck I was going to sing to Scratch's playing.

"Please," I whisper-begged so no one else could hear. "Please, Scratch, what was that song you were playing? I couldn't figure it out, so I couldn't sing it. What was it?"

"How should I know?" he said calmly. "You gonna finish that banana?"

"Here, have the banana. Now tell me what words to sing when you play."

"Sing whatever words you want," he said as he shoved the whole banana into his mouth. "It's all the same to me."

"Thanks, Scratch, you're a big help. How am I going to figure out . . . hey, you know you're not supposed to eat . . . you know the peel of the banana is kind of . . . fine, Scratch, eat the peel."

Great help he was, but what can you expect from a guy who eats the skin off his food and the leather off the steering wheel, and sprouts? I saw him one day, actually eating sprouts. "And maybe you could change those pants one of these days, huh, Scratch," I said as I moved off to find somebody helpful. "They're starting to get pretty shiny there."

"They're vinyl pants. They're supposed to be shiny."

It was starting to erode my brain, hanging with these guys. Like standing in front of a leaky microwave all day long.

"Now, what we do in south Alabama," Cecil said, picking up on my problem, "is, practically everybody writes their own songs. And it don't make no difference what the tune is. If you've ever been to a barn dance you can figure out how to fit the words to it. Should I show you?"

No. Now this was simply going too far. I had to draw the line somewhere. I had my dignity, after all. The answer was no.

Probably. What good would it do me to listen to Cleetus here singing about I'm so lonesome I could hug a chicken? I mean . . .

Hey, that's not bad. Maybe not a chicken, but close. Hmmm.

"All right, I got no time for pride right now, I've got to catch a rocket to stardom. Educate me."

"Sure then, you go like this: If they're playin' it fast, you gotta sing about fast stuff, which means (a) your car, (b) your lifestyle, (c) your old girl-friend, who ain't no good. Now, on the other hand, if they're playin' it nice and gentle, then you got to sing about nice stuff and gentle stuff like (a) your dead dog, (b) huntin', or (c) your new girlfriend who is like an angel straight outta heaven."

The question was, was stardom really worth this?

"Don't tell me any more, Festus," I said. "I think I'm gonna puke."

"Naw, you just don't know what it sounds like yet, that's all."

He took a couple of lungfuls of air, preparing to demonstrate.

"No!" I yelled, stopping him just in time, before god-knows-what came out of him. "Let's just go up there and surprise ourselves, shall we? It'll be more fun if we don't know too much ahead of time."

Cecil beamed at the thought. "You are fully correct," he said. "That will be more fun. I gotta tell you, Wolf, you are, every day, the most fun feller I have ever met."

I shook my head at him. "Killer," I said, "I cannot even imagine what kind of a sorry life you must have led back there in Alabama."

When we reassembled to make musical history, we were ready. Scratch had fortified himself with all the nutritional items a garage had to offer—some loose bolts, a fan belt, a can of 10W-30 motor oil. Jerome and Steven had spent the break spitting at each other over the band's percussion philosophy. (Jerome: "Don't *tell* me when to hit my triangle, Steven. *I* will decide when the song needs a *ping*, and if I think it needs one every two seconds, then I will *ping* my brains out." Steven: "Fine, Jerome, if you want every six-year-old in the city to come running every time we play because they think we're a stupid ice-cream truck.") Ling had set his bass drum and stool up on top of a stack of pallets, and was practicing a very cool unsmiling nod to the crowd.

And of course, the Singer was ready now, without a song.

We all stared at each other for a while.

"So," Jerome said. "How do we start?"

"Jeez," Cecil marveled, "this bunch really is starting from scratch, huh?"

"Har-har," Scratch said.

Cecil was already falling behind. "What? What'd I say?"

"Nevermind," I said. "But he's right, Scratch. You go. We'll follow."

I thought now I might be able to sneak this one

through. "So, which song are we going to start with?"

He shrugged. "The fast one."

And that's what it was. In fact, that was about all it was. Scratch ripped into the music like he was peeling away from the line in a drag race.

Steven jumped on, *snappety snappety snappety snappety*.

Ling listened, nodded, nodded, started banging, *boom buboom boom buboom*.

Ting.

Lars did his thing, which, I hate to admit, was the real thing, an instrument playing a tune, with notes and a structure. He worked up a rhythm that Cecil then imitated on his washboard. Our lead guitarist was still out there on an untethered walk in space, but we had our group noise going, and this appeared to be where I came in.

"Go, Wolf," Jerome called.

"Ya," said Steven. "If you can't keep up, Wonder Wheels, pull over into the breakdown lane."

He said it really loud, too. Terrible things were happening here, and I don't mean the music—though that was terrible enough. I think it was the drum making Steven so bold and clever. It was the big bass making Ling into a cross between Michael Jackson and Boris the Dancing Bear. Even Lars, who was such a wonk before he strapped on his Fender . . . okay, bad example, but anyway, these guys were all gaining power while I was being drained of mine because . . . because . . .

Because of my little secret problem.

"Join the party," Cecil hooted. "The music shall set you free."

"Maybe I don't want to be free," I said, rapidly losing my nerve. I tapped the microphone lightly with my index finger. It sounded like thunder.

Scratch played harder, harder, wilder. Everybody followed him.

"You don't even know what you're playing," I scolded them all over the P.A. "You're making fools of yourselves, I must tell you."

I don't even think they were listening to me at this point. (And from the sound of it they definitely weren't listening to each other.) They were all off in their own spaces, bearing down on their instruments, flogging the entire history of music into submission.

And loving the bejesus out of it.

So who slipped me the kryptonite? What had happened to the Wolf we had all grown to know and fear and respect and emulate and love? (Well, all the other stuff, anyway.) What was missing here?

"Hey," Steven called above the din. He waved me over toward him with one drumstick while he flailed away aimlessly with the other.

Reluctantly, sheepishly, I answered his summons—which is how you could tell that I was simply not right. When I'd wheeled up close to where he was sitting, he grabbed the microphone out of my hand.

"Lemme show you," he said, laughing. Then he shrieked his song into the mike:

> *Oh, Wolf-o's scared witless what He-*
> *Men'll think,*
> *He can't make no music 'cause he's such*
> *a dink. . . .*

"Gimme that!" I growled, clutching at the microphone while the rest of them laughed. Steven held the thing up high out of my reach. Then he yelped some more:

> *We'll really know all, when we hear*
> *Wolfman sing,*
> *We blew it last time*
> *We should have voted for Ling. . . .*

I punched him so hard in the stomach that you could hear his intestines go *squish* over the microphone.

And it was good.

Problem was, he was right. How long could I keep my affliction hidden? I couldn't let them see it.

Everyone was laughing and hooting now. The force of the punch caused me to wheel backward ten feet across the garage. I swaggered back toward Steven (it's hard to describe how a guy swaggers in a wheelchair, but I've mastered it, you'll have to take my word) and snatched *my* microphone.

Now I knew what I'd lost temporarily. My fangs. Thanks, Steve-o.

"*Hel-looo baayyyyyyybeeee,*" I sang over the sound system. "*Now my wheels be fast and my woman be trashed and I got no cash but I gotalotta flash and yo' momma think I'm brash, but Sir Chesthair gonna crash . . .*"

Oh yes. The Wolf had returned. It was time to howl.

7
Backstage Passes

Once we launched the Sniffs, we became the busiest band in the biz. We played the sidewalk in front of the subway hole where I first discovered Scratch. ("Ah, the memories," he said as some guy threw an apple core into our pass-the-hat hat. No problem, though, as Scratch ate the core and Ling just put the hat right back on.) We played in front of the Goodwill collection bins in the Buddy's Liquors parking lot. ("I'll take that hat, lady," said Ling. "No kidding," Scratch said, fondling a very soft and worn-out single driving glove, "real leather, you say, huh? You sure you don't want this?" It was our most lucrative gig.)

The beauty of it was, we were getting famous—a little—we were profiting—a little—and all the while we weren't getting one lick better. In fact, I believe we got worse the more we played together.

The sound we made as a unit was the most glorious annoyance imaginable.

I was in heaven.

"But maybe we don't want to play for apples and pennies and people's old underwear," Steven said as we were hauling our stuff back to the club following a blistering set outside the Peaceable Kingdom pet store. ("See," said Scratch. "I always knew these bone-shaped cookies had to be tasty, but nobody would listen." "No, sir, I don't know what a tick dip is," said Cecil, "but if it's free and you think I could use one, I'll take it. Thank ya kindly.")

"Ya, mister *man*ager," Jerome said. Jerome was getting to be one feisty little triangulist. "I think it's about time you improved the quality of our venues."

"Venues . . ." Lars said. "Ah, that means songs, right? He wants us to play better songs?"

"Places," Scratch answered. "Jerome is suggesting we move up to classier shows, and I think he's right. We're ready, Wolf. Except for maybe . . . one or two adjustments." As he said that, Scratch aimed his guitar at Lars like a machine gun. Lars, oblivious, just went on turning the tuning keys on his guitar, which he did all the time and which really bothered the rest of us, who did no such thing.

Tuning, don't you hate that?

"I know," I said to Scratch. "You and I will have a musical strategy meeting after we adjourn the general meeting—"

"Is this a meeting?" Ling asked as he sweated under the hot sun with the bass drum and my sound system on his back. "It doesn't feel like a meeting. Look, my makeup is starting to run."

That's right. His stage makeup. And it was running. Ling-Ling's eye and cheek colors were beginning to melt, and if you think he was a sight before, picture him with his doughy face curdling and dissolving.

"Okay," I said as we broke through the door into the cool of Lars's garage. "Everybody just dump your gear and call it a day. Scratch and me are going to hash a couple of things out, and then, by the time you all return on Monday, we will have a couple of announcements regarding our next, fantabulous show, and the course of our rise to fame thereafter."

"Wow," said Cecil. "Those are some excellent words. I can't wait."

"Ya, well, wait anyway," Steven advised. "Because

the most excellent word of all for our manager is *Crockasaurus*."

"*Rock*-a-saurus," I corrected. "See you all on Monday. Rest up; you were brilliant today. You killed 'em. Keep the edge, keep the edge."

The He-Men filed out, dreaming of greatness to come, I'm sure.

It was my job to dream up the how part.

I knew where to start. I didn't know much else, but I knew where to start.

"Hey, Lars," I said as he climbed into his jump-suit to get back to the day job he hardly ever did anymore. He was getting like an irresponsible kid, shirking all his chores to chase a fantasy that made no sense. "Got a minute there, Lars?"

"Right then," Lars croaked in a fake Cockney accent. "What can I do you blokes for?"

"The blokes want you out," I blurted.

"Let him down easy, wouldja?" Scratch whispered.

"Oh," I said. "Well, take all the time you need clearing out your corner of the arena. And whenever you want to come see us play, you're in for backstage passes."

"You're a sport," Scratch said.

"What, backstage passes, I *own* the stage,

remember? So just forget about it. I'm not leaving. What do you think of that?"

Mind you, this was the one *adult* in the group.

"I'll just hang around, and whenever you play, I'll play louder. If you go on the road, I'll follow."

I turned to Scratch, giving him the "What now?" face.

"All right," Scratch said, trying to relate to Lars in a language I didn't speak—guitar. "But you gotta sloppy it up. You gotta stop trying to make songs where there are none. You gotta be a mess like the rest of us, otherwise you're destroying our distinctive sound."

"I'll do it, I will," Lars promised, desperate not to lose his shot at fame. "I'll go put my axe way out of tune right now."

"That's a start," I said. "Run along."

Cecil walked back in through the door he'd walked out of ten minutes before.

"No," I explained to him slowly. "You see, Cleetus, if you turn right at *every* corner, you wind up back where you started."

"I forgot I had some work to do," he answered.

"Work? What kind of work would you have?"

I could see out of the corner of my eye as Scratch began waving his hands in an X pattern in front of his face like a railroad crossing sign. I spun—my famous one-hand, one-wheel, quick turn—to catch him.

"And *why* shouldn't he tell me?" I asked. "Am I *not* the president of this club?"

"Dictator . . ." Scratch muttered out of one side of his mouth.

"And am I *not* manager of the Sniffs?"

"Dictator . . ." he repeated.

"He's building a platform for me," Lars said, creeping back to life and back into the mix. "So I can play from up—"

"For you?" Scratch asked. "I thought he was making a platform for me! This is *Scratch* and the Sniffs, after all. . . ."

The Killer was beaming. "Y'see, boss, I was talkin' before and I let slip how I was handy with wood . . ." His voice trailed off and up at the end of the sentence as if he was asking a question. ". . . and about how when my uncle Redale an' me built a silo just the two of us in one weekend, and it still stood up even when a tornado picked it up an' dropped it, and even no matter how many times ol' Redale banged into it with his tractor—"

"Whoa, whoa," I cut in. "You guys are contracting individually to have your own little stages

58

made? How pathetic. How slimy. How foolish and vain and misguided. You guys make me sick."

I grabbed Cecil by the elbow. "How big? However high you make theirs, you have to make mine a few inches higher. Listen to ol' Wolf. I control the purse strings around here, you know. . . ."

"Y'*all* make me wanna shout," Cecil growled. "I never saw such a crew. We are a team. A unit. None of us is any greater or lesser than any of the others."

"Sure, *you'd* like to believe that." I laughed.

"Shaddup, for once," Lars said.

"Ya," Scratch joined. "Give it a rest, ya mean little monster."

The room went dead. Now, I certainly appreciate the old give-and-take as much as the next He-Man—okay, a little more than the next He-Man—but a line had been crossed here.

I knew what was there, between the lines of that phrase, *ya little monster*. You spend most of your life in a wheelchair, and certain patterns emerge that you can recognize easily. I know that I leave myself open for such things, and that maybe there isn't a great well of sympathy out there for the likes of me, but still . . .

"That was cold, man," I said quietly, my voice

59

trembling a bit. I turned and wheeled myself toward the door.

Cecil caught me just before I got outside.

"Hey, Wolf. That wasn't right. Everybody knows it. Everybody's sorry."

"They all say that?" I asked.

"Well, no. But I think they think it."

I wheeled on.

"Don't leave. We need you. And I won't let nobody pull that kind of stuff on you again. Not while The Killer's around. I promise."

I looked up at that long country mile of Cecil towering over me and gave him my most spectacular pitiful Tiny Tim face.

"Will you," I sniffed, "build me a platform higher than the ones you're building for the rest of them?"

He sighed, looked over his shoulder to where the two guitarists were bonding once more. "Okay, but just a little higher. Just a little ol' bitty bit."

Do you love him? Do you just love him?

Cecil started wheeling me back to the other guys. "And you'll make me a ramp, so I can get up and down from my platform easily?"

"Oh, I'd 'spect that would be some kind of law, that if I built you something it would have to be handicapped accessible."

"True," I piped. "That's very true. And we wouldn't want to get you in trouble for breaking any city ordinances so soon after arriving in town. I couldn't allow that, Cecil."

"You're a good man, Wolf."

He said that, he really did. I couldn't make that up.

8

The Devil in White Bucks

I was lying in bed thinking hard about what I was going to tell the guys on Monday. How in the world was I going to get a better gig than the one at the Goodwill box? Where do you go from there? What more do they want from me? I'm only human, after all. I'm only one man. . . .

"I don't care how many men you are, it's time to turn out the lights," the screw said, poking his head into my unit.

"Oh, was I thinking out loud?"

"That would be a pleasant change," he answered.

I hate wiseguys. Don't you hate wiseguys? Anyway, he wasn't a screw exactly, he was more of a monitor at the facility where I live. And it's not a very harsh environment, just between you and me.

"Harvey," I told him. "Harvey, you run this joint like a prison."

"Write to your congressman."

"I did. He sent me a picture of himself."

"There. So quit your bellyaching."

"Harvey, I have an idea."

"I got no money, Wolfgang."

"It's not one of those ideas . . . exactly. I want you to let my band play here."

"Here? In your bedroom?"

"No, here, in the rec room."

Harvey thought about it, pulled the cap off his bald head, scratched, put the cap back on. He came in and sat on the edge of the bed, exhausted from the effort of scratching. "What kind of music you play?"

"We . . . um . . ."

He had me there.

"Wolf, you even got a band? C'mon, I told you, I got no money."

"It's not a scam. We play, sort of, punk-jug music."

"Punk-j—? I see. Listen, it sounds cute. You don't play too loud, clean up after yourselves, and I suppose you can have the room to yourselves on Saturday afternoon for an hour or so."

I shook my head at him.

"No? What, no?"

"No, we are not cute—*boy* are we not cute—and no, we don't just want the room. It has to be a show. With some people to hear us. And . . . you gotta pay us."

"I gotta . . . pay? Turn off your light and go to bed."

"I'm serious. Just pay us something, anything, and we'll put on a show for the whole joint. It'll be worth it. Everybody'll love ya. We got seven guys. Give us, oh, two bucks a head, fourteen dollars. It's a steal—and it'll keep me from stealing."

Harvey shook his head, looked at his watch. "At least I still got my watch," he said. "Whenever I have dealings with you . . ." He cut himself off in mid-insult. He pointed at me and smiled.

"Okay," he said. "But I got a condition."

"Of course you do," I said. "I wouldn't respect you if you didn't have a condition."

"I play a pretty peppy accordion. . . ."

Oh my god . . .

"The good news," I announced to the assembled He-Men on Monday, "is that we've got our break-out concert."

The He-Men went wild, like on those nature programs when the nest of gorillas all try to scare the cameraman away, beating on their chests, screeching, slapping the ground with their big hairy hands.

"The bad news is, we got another geezer on board."

"What kind of geezer?" Jerome asked.

"Ah, the accordion-playing kind."

The He-Men all went wild again.

"Come on, guys, all we got to do is let him sit in for a couple of minutes, we'll drown him out, and he won't be a problem anymore. We humor him a little, then ignore him, like we do with Lars."

"Hey," yelled Lars.

"See that," I said. "I can't even tell when Lars is with us anymore."

Then I told them where we'd be playing.

"Really broke your neck over the weekend finding us a place to play, huh, Wolf?" Steven said. "What'd you do, just roll out of bed one morning and . . ."

Should I tell him that I didn't even roll out of bed? Probably not, huh?

They muttered, they conferred, they huddled without me.

"And they're paying us two bucks a head."

The murmurs turned to low oohhs and hums of

approval. It doesn't matter that it's not much; if somebody's paying you to do a thing, it's a much cooler thing. I had them now.

"Hey, it's two thirty-three a head if we cut Lars out."

As manager, it was a relatively easy gig to prepare for. I was fairly familiar with the location. The commute to the venue was pretty easy. And the audience was ready-made and more or less captive. My preparations as singer, on the other hand . . .

We'd made a crude tape on Lars's big old stereo, the one that doubled as my sound system. Back at the home, I took the tape and popped it into the cassette deck in my room. I sat and I listened.

I turned the tape up as loud as it could go.

I snapped it back off.

"What was that?" I asked the deck. That wasn't us. That couldn't have been us.

I turned the tape back on again, lower volume.

There was Scratch's crazy guitar. There was Lars trying to follow him. Could be us, I guess. And . . . yes, that sounded like Ling's bass boom. And the tom-tom, tom-*tom*-tom/tom-*tom*-tom (I *hate* Wolf/I *hate* Wolf), that was very Steven. And the jug. Is that a jug sound in there?

Ping . . . one-two-three . . . *ting* . . . one-two-three.

Yup, that was us. If there was one element that separated us from your average meat-grinder punk-rock outfit, it was probably Jerome's tidy triangle.

But what was missing from this sonic picture?

I had to try. I had to work it out. They were right, all right? I had to admit that I, Wolfgang Amadeus Rivera, was afraid of music. Or at least, I was afraid of what came out when I tried to make any.

As I mentioned, I had a condition. A fearsome condition.

I know. Me and fear, they just don't go together. I'm as surprised as you are.

I went to the mirror. Stared myself down.

Look at me, wouldja? With a face like that, what am I worried about?

Music on. I start snapping my fingers. Music up louder. Jeez, they are awfully screechy. I snap louder. Two-hand snapping. I unbutton two buttons on my shirt. Resume snapping. Allow a small, one-sided smile. A sneer. Raise one eyebrow. Focus the Stare, so I'm looking down *on* the audience, rather than at them. We are not friends. We are not peers. We are not equals. You, audience, are here to worship me, and I, idol, am here to let you. And to sing.

The band behind me was in full gale now, the force of them blowing my hair out of place, which we cannot have. I reslick the hair. The guys sound like they are in mortal combat with their instruments. The video to this song would look like a battle scene from *Braveheart.*

My entrance.

" '*Rocky Mountain High/Colorado—*' "

No, no. Please.

" '*What's new pussycat/Whoa whoa whoa whoa whoa—*' "

Not.

" '*A white/sport coat/and a pink/car-nation . . .*' "

Oh my god, oh my god! It's true. Worst fears, worst fears realized. Code red. No—code, code black or whatever the worst code is. Life is over!

There's a dweeb trapped inside me and it's gonna come out when I try to sing in front of people!!!!!!!!!!!!!!!!!!!!!!!!!!

I had some perverse natural attraction to the entire catalog of the geek anthems and weenie singers of history. Pat Boone, Donny Osmond, Paul McCartney, Michael Bolton. They all live up there in my head like an army of tiny devils using midget paintbrushes to paint my brain with syrup. They killed me with that stuff in therapy, hoping to smother my antisocial tendencies, and it stuck!

Now my secret would come out.

I just have to do the honorable and sensible thing. I don't have a sword handy, so I'll just take this cassette player with me into the bathroom, fill the tub, and jump. I have no choice. Steven will have me for lunch the minute the boys go into their thrash routine and I break out with something from *Cats*.

The music throbbed on as I stared at the simp in the mirror. God, we had a serious drum attack when you really listened. Maybe I should just go all the way, put on the black horn-rim glasses, slip a pocket protector and some pens in my shirt pocket . . . listen to those drums.

Listen to Steven. When did *he* get so powerful?

Tom-*tom*-tom,tom-*tom*-tom . . .

(Wolf-is-a-goof, is-a-goof, is-a-goof. . . .)

No way. I could beat this. Stare, Wolfgang. Beat this. No way, Steve-o.

I just had to stop thinking about the therapy. Think antisocial thoughts, think antisocial.

There was only one way. If I was going to wind up sounding like Wolf, there was only one song-writer I could depend on.

Wolf.

9
Sniffomania

Guys like me have a lot more friends than you probably think. To tell you the truth, it turned out that guys like me have a lot more friends than I myself thought.

On Friday night, an hour before we were supposed to play, the rec room was packed. Harvey, who had decided to charge four bits a head ("Hey, it's charity"), was making a killing. He scrambled all over the building collecting gray metal folding chairs to stuff more paying bodies into the room, and when those ran out, he actually upped the price for standing room tickets.

"Why do I gotta pay seventy-five cents to stand up," one rough-looking patron asked, "when they get to sit for fifty cents?"

"Because you can see the stage," Harvey answered, "and the seats are obstructed view."

"Cool," the guy said.

"And if you're standing, you get better leverage when it's time to throw stuff."

"Hey," I yelled from the stage, where we were setting up.

"Just a joke," Harvey said, coming right up on-stage with us. He dropped his peppy accordion down in front. "They're gonna love you guys. They don't get much pleasure in their lives."

"Oh, that's good to know," Jerome said nervously. "At least you know these guys, right? I mean, they're your people, so they won't act up or anything."

"Jerome," I sighed. "There are eighteen people living in this home. There are about sixty in the audience."

"Seventy-three," Harvey said as he sat on the floor making little stacks of coins.

"Where'd you get them all?" I asked.

"Some of them are guests of the residents. But then I got a great idea and called some of my colleagues. We bussed in kids from the really wicked facilities across town. They were starved for entertainment."

"Oh my god, oh my god," Jerome moaned. "We have to escape. We're surrounded by criminals."

71

"They're not *crim*inals," I assured my increasingly worried-looking bandmates. "They're people with issues, that's all."

"Just like yourself?" asked Steven. He was not trying to be helpful.

"Yes, exactly," I said, falling for it.

They all started packing up again.

"Stop it now," I demanded. I looked at King Harvey's growing money pile. "Four bucks. Double time. Everybody gets four bucks."

They stopped packing. Harvey looked up at me and scowled.

"Ya?" I said to him. "You want us to leave, and let you and your peppy accordion amuse the people with the issues?"

"Fine," he said. "But no more raises."

"And don't forget," I added, as we got set up for good, "it's four sixty-six if we cut out Lars."

"You can't cut me out; I need this money bad. I'm not working on cars anymore."

"That's how you can tell we've made it as musicians," Scratch joked. "We're all broke."

And it went like that for a while. We got closer, the bunch of us, as a creeping nervousness overtook us. The customers kept pouring in; the sweatiness of the room built. The crowd got edgy.

It rumbled. The band got edgy. We joked.

"Here are some important tips," I said, addressing the group with my back to the audience. "The first thing is, don't provoke them."

"Oh, I feel better already," Jerome said.

"How would we provoke them?" Ling asked from behind the world's largest pair of rectangular mirrored sunglasses. It looked like he had the John Hancock Building hanging off his face.

"Well, if we stink, for instance," I said. "That would probably provoke them."

"That's it, we're dead," Jerome said.

"Why? Why is that?" Cecil wanted to know.

"Wake up, will you, Hopalong?" said Steven. "We do stink. Everybody knows we stink. *We* know we stink. That's part of our charm."

"Right," Lars said. "Like the Pistols."

"If he says that one more time . . ." Ling said, raising a drumstick in a rare outburst of emotion.

"Layyydies annnnd *gen*tlemen," Harvey screamed over the crowd noise. They were still coming in as he introduced us. "Have we got a trrrrreat for you now."

Like the hardened professionals we were, each one of us froze solid at the sound of the show starting. Except Scratch, who dropped automatically into I'm-so-cool-I-don't-even-hear-anybody mode. I was off to the side a bit, stage right, so I could wheel in and make a splash at the right time. Ling and Steven clustered in the back the way well-trained drummers are supposed to, and the guitarists stood opposite me on the left wing. Behind me on one side was The Killer, warming up the old washboard, and on the other side, hanging precariously close to the front of the stage, was the King of Ting himself, Jerome.

Just before Harvey blew the starting gun, a girl came up close. It was not as if it was a real stage that could truly separate (protect?) us from adoring fans. It was only two feet up from the rest of the floor, and was usually used for the monthly speeches we got from the state communicable disease guy (who was always good for a laugh) and the free poetry readings (which were even funnier).

But it was not just any girl, creeping up closer and closer, going all dewy-eyed and goofy. It was Vanessa, a.k.a. "Ness the Mess" or "Loch Ness," a nine-year-old, three-foot-tall plug of a stout thing. She was also the only sister of one of our most frightening neighbors here at the home, Von.

So, Von's sister, Nessy, shouldered her way to

the front, clearly under the spell of the rock-and-roll god. And who could blame her? I was prepared for this. I might as well get used to it if I was going to be in this racket. The trick is to be just charming enough so you don't hurt their feelings—and so they *do* continue to spend their money on your music—but not so charming that they start stalking you.

"Well, hello there, Vanessa," I said, wheeling right to the edge of the stage. "Are you ready for the big—"

Her eyes, normally a stunning yellow, had gone almost totally black with the intensity of her passion. She looked like a steroid-pumped sprinter in the starting blocks.

"Who is he?" she gasped. "I want to know who he is."

She was pointing at our little Jerome.

"You're joking," I said.

"I don't joke," Vanessa said in a very serious tone.

"You're joking," Jerome said, in a far more serious one.

I started laughing right out loud as Jerome scuttled around behind me and Vanessa made like she was going to mount the stage right there. I looked back over my shoulder to see Dr. J holding his tambourine up like a shield.

"Gonna have to do better than that, Jerome," I said. "She's a stocky little thing."

"Oh my god, oh my god," he said. "Wolf, get her away from me. You're the singer. You're the He-Man president. Do something."

" 'Scuse me, missy," I said, holding out my hands to ward her off. "But I'm afraid we cannot allow anyone on the stage. Why, if we let every girl who wanted a piece of He-Man Jerome—"

"Eeeeeeeee!" she screamed when I said his name.

So I did it again. "After the show, Jerome will—"

"Eeeeeee!"

I spun around and shook his hand. "Nothing I can do there, old dog. You got yourself a groupie already."

"Oh my god, oh my god." Nervously, spastically, Jerome started whacking away at his cymbal. The rest of the band took it as a cue, and chopped into a songlike thing.

Von stepped right up to the stage, put one hand on the shoulder of his sister, and pointed with the other hand at Jerome, who was all of three feet away.

Have I mentioned that Von is very protective of his sister?

"I'n gone keel you," Von said to Jerome in his one-of-a-kind Von dialect.

Jerome couldn't even manage to say "oh my god." He bit his lips and banged nervously away on his instruments as Von folded his arms and planted himself, and Nessy mooned over Jerome.

". . . So now give us some *big* noise clapping for . . . Scratch and the Sniffs!"

10
Gotta Be Me

You couldn't tell from the sound of us that we hadn't really rehearsed the whole week before the show. Then again, you couldn't tell if we had, either. The band was simply on fire right from the start, with Scratch in particular bouncing unbelievable, pointless riffs off the walls, the percussionists matching him, and the whole mishmash meeting in the middle of the room where the crowd made a spontaneous mosh pit.

"More!" somebody screamed from the front row. What was that supposed to mean? Shouldn't you wait till the band stops before you demand more?

"Louder!" came another scream, then another. The guys gave them louder.

"Louder!" they screamed.

"More!"

Fortunately, Sniffomaniacs are not very complicated or demanding creatures.

"Louder, we can give," Steven called out, beating the tom-tom and laughing.

"And more," Ling said. He scanned the room, his glasses reflecting every gold tooth and silver skull pinkie ring. "We can manage 'more.'"

"Ya," I said. "Let's just hope nobody calls for 'better.'"

I noticed that our friends were enjoying themselves immensely. Almost enjoying themselves *too* much, you might say.

Was that a punch?

No, my mistake. They're dancing.

Hey, should they really be holding her up that high, especially as she appears not to like it so much?

Oo, a little blood there. Somebody caught a stray elbow, that's all. Boys will be—

"Hey," I said, "let go. Ya, you down there. Let go. Let go of that wheel, I said. Stop it."

"Yo, Wolfie, we just figured as long as you're gonna sit there like a spectator, you might as well be down here like one."

"Good point!" yelled Steven.

"Hey," I yelled. "I got a job here."

"You sellin' popcorn?"

"I'm the singer," I said with great authority.

"If you're the singer, then how come you don't sing?"

This was getting tight.

Steven the Johnny Rotten Chesthair trouble-maker raised his arms high above his head, and started smacking his drumsticks together, inciting the very incitable crowd. "Wolf-gang! Wolf-gang! Wolf-gang! Wolf-gang!"

Everybody in the room picked up the chant. Almost.

"Jeroooome!" squealed Vanessa.

"I'n gone keel you," added Von.

"Shaddup, all of ya," I screamed over the micro-phone. Harvey had allowed us to use the official Division of Social Services speaker system, so I sounded like authority. "I'll sing when I *feel* like it. If I even feel like it at all."

"Booo!" they said. "Boooo!" But I think it was more like the way people in other countries whistle when they don't like a performance. This booing didn't mean they weren't having a good time. These people *liked* to boo.

"Boo to you too," I snarled. "I ain't singing. So go on home, ya criminal slobs."

I know these types. You have to show them who's boss. If you don't, they'll walk all over you.

Or they'll pick you up by your wheelchair and carry you all around the room.

"Put me down!" I hollered. "I mean it. Don't you make me come down out of this chair and give you a whipping."

You'd have thought I was a comic rather than a singer the way they all shrieked at me.

"All right then, you asked for it." I stuck two fingers in my mouth and blew until my ears popped, whistling loud enough to bring St. Bernards down from the Alps. "Yo, He-Men, come on down here and help me out. Show these chumps . . ."

Scratch, working on an especially indecipherable guitar figure, called, "Be with you in a minute, man." The original, charter-member He-Men? Nothing.

The Killer, though, was his true-blue self. Cecil threw both his jug and his washboard over his shoulder, narrowly missing Ling-Ling, and charged into the hostile crowd.

But he might as well have been one of those oversize beach balls they pass around the bleachers at baseball games. Poor Cecil was airborne practically before he'd even left the stage. He looked so confused by all this.

"What does this mean?" he asked as we passed

each other, traveling in opposite directions at the rear of the room. "Is it that they like us, or they don't?"

"Just lie back and enjoy the ride." I sighed. Then I looked back to the stage, where Jerome was mouthing "Help me," while Vanessa played with his shoelaces.

"That's it," I commanded from my throne high above the demented rabble. "You want me to sing, you betcha I'll sing. I'm gonna mop the joint with you slugs. Take me to the stage." I pointed the way, looking like George Washington crossing the Delaware. "I'm gonna sing, and boy are you going to be sorry."

That was all they needed. They couldn't ferry me back to the stage fast enough then. Once there, I sat, glaring out over them. Cecil was still traveling the room like a cloud. "And I need him back here," I demanded. "I can't sing without my jug player."

Cecil, being without a wheelchair, was delivered to the stage much more quickly than I was. In fact, he flew the last ten feet when they tossed him in a mighty heave right up at my feet.

"Thanks for makin' 'em put me back," Cecil said from his position flat out on the floor.

We were all in position, a tight unit once more. I felt stronger now, knowing all my boys were behind me.

"Well, if you're not gonna sing, maybe you should try dancing," Steven yelled.

Okay, *some* of my boys were behind me. Anyway, they were very loud, which was what mattered most.

Okay, Wolf, this is your moment. Remember, just be you, just be you. Don't be the geek. Just be yourself, and it'll all work. Ready . . . Set . . . Be yourself.

" 'Whether I'm right . . .' "

Oh, cripes no, not this.

" 'Or whether I'm wrong . . .' "

That's it, my life is over. The Wolf is dead. Long live Mister Velvet.

" 'Whether I find my place in this world, or just never belong . . .

" 'I gotta be meeeeeee . . .

" 'I've just gotta be me . . .' "

I closed my eyes as my stupid mouth went on singing. I think I even did that goofy swinging the microphone by the handle move that all the blow-dry singers do.

Even as my body went on acting the fool without

my consent, I sat there and waited for merciful death to come. But with the band wailing behind me, sounding like a circus calliope being run over by a tractor-trailer, I couldn't hear the audience response.

I sure could feel it, though.

Something hit me, which was not surprising. I opened my eyes to find it was a pair of underwear. They were Calvin Kleins, so I couldn't tell if they were guys' or girls', but because the faces in front of me were smiling, the hands were waving, and the bodies were dancing, I figured it was a friendly pair of underwear either way.

They loved us.

"Can you believe this?" Cecil said, screaming in my ear. He was also blowing into his jug between words and beating himself on the head with his washboard. Our drummers had caught such a fever they sounded like the whole Navajo nation. Scratch had jumped down into the crowd and was letting anyone who wanted to have a whack at the strings, and it didn't change his sound in the slightest.

As I saw Harvey cheering, clapping, and approaching the stage, I reached behind me and lifted the accordion. I held it high like a sacrifice I was going to heave into a volcano, and I handed it to the crowd.

"Good-bye, peppy accordion," I said as the instrument rode the wave over the crowd and then was swallowed. Harvey was likewise swallowed as he chased it.

I looked off to my left and there was Vanessa, pointing at herself, then at Jerome, then herself, then Jerome. You get the picture.

Then Von started. Pointed at himself, then at Jerome, then himself, then Jerome.

Every one of our players was playing his heart out, and the assembled sound was . . .

Hideous.

We made the most obnoxious noise in the history of ears, and people worshipped us for it. They gave us money. They threw underwear at us. It was like poking someone in the eye over and over and having them pay you and ask for more.

I felt so dirty about the whole thing.

Heh-heh.

"You like that one?" I screamed, my confidence growing now like some fiendish evil green lab experiment run amok. "Well, then, suck on this one."

And into the mix I flew, sounding just as out of

place with the thrash and grind of the Sniffs as I could.

"*'I write the songs that make the whole world sing. . . .'*"

Delirium. I didn't know how long I could hold this group together. They were slamming into each other pretty good down there on the dance floor.

"*'If you get caught between the moon and New York City . . .'*"

Somebody threw a battery. Then somebody threw a chair. Scratch tried to get back up onstage, but they wouldn't give him back.

"Harvey!" I screamed.

Cecil threw himself once more into the tussle. Steven followed. They got sucked up like they were in a giant human food processor. Harvey emerged talking into his handset, and his assistants came running into the room. Vanessa took advantage of the situation to hop up onstage. Exit one triangle player out the back door like a fox terrier into a hollow log.

So I was there, and Lars was there—petrified, like a statue of his goofy self. And Ling was still there, laying down the beat.

Harvey was making a slashing motion across his throat, trying to get me to stop.

"What, are you kidding?" I said into the microphone. "I'm just getting warm. Make them sit down so I can sing some more."

Harvey's mouth hung open. He didn't need to say anything. Make them sit down? I was one of them, I knew better than that.

But I had the bug.

"*We had joy, we had fun, we had seasons in the sun . . .*"

It was almost a cappella, with Ling-Ling now reduced to beating out the tune with one stick while he waved to the audience with the other. But we were enough.

Suddenly the power went out.

"Show's over," Harvey screamed over the sound of breaking glass.

I must say in defense of our fans that though they may have been a little destructive, they were clearly not mean-spirited. They were having a fine time.

"Everybody out!"

And with that, we, Scratch and the Sniffs, were herded up and pushed toward the door, to give everybody the message.

"The Sniffs have left the building," Harvey announced from the stage, even though everyone could see we were still there.

As I was wheeled away, I was rushed by the neighborhood's really *big* businessman—he weighed about four hundred pounds—Sammy Blue. Sammy was always into something—caramel hot dog stands, local boxing promotion, designer dog breeding. Bright, lucrative ideas nobody else had.

"You a genius, boy," Sammy said, pumping my hand. "A bona fide musical genius. The way you combined the different genres there—how many genres did you have going there anyway, seven, eight?"

"Twelve," I said coolly, making a mental note to look up *musical genres* in the Funk & Wagnalls later on.

"We gotta talk," Sammy said. "Can we talk?"

"I don't know if you can talk," I said, "but everybody knows I can."

11
Just Don't Think About It

"Would I lie?"

It was a rhetorical question, but with a straight-shootin' buck like Cecil, a question's a question.

"I believe you would, yes," he said.

"Well, I'm not lying. Sammy Blue wants us to make a music video, and that's the straight stuff."

We were gathered for a super-secret session of the He-Man Women Haters Club, called by me to discuss this major break in our careers. We sat in and around the black Lincoln—just like in the old days when we were simple common peasants like the rest of you.

"We're going to be on MTV," Ling sang, jamming both drumsticks in the air. He carried them with him everywhere now.

"I'm not going on MTV," Jerome said from his hiding spot under the dashboard. I peeked in at him. He looked like a bony Chihuahua shivering after a bath. "I'm not going anywhere, ever again. She's out there. She's going to get me. The last thing I want to do is go out and flaunt myself in front of her anymore."

"Hey, I forgot about you, ya big love monkey, you," I said.

"Don't call me that," he yipped. "We're supposed to be the Women *Haters*, remember?"

"Ah, that's just a saying," I answered. "We don't really mean it."

"Oh yes we do," Steven cut in.

Now, why is it that the guys who actually have the girls chasing after them are the ones who want to hate 'em the most? Ain't that peculiar?

"Listen, you, we can't have that stuff right now. We need you to be at your Johnny Chesthairiest for this operation. Because like it or not, and as big a mystery as it is to me, in this group you are the Cute One. Blecchh."

He smiled at that. "Say it again."

"Excuse me?"

"Say it again, so I'm sure I got it right. What's my job again?"

Now, what could possibly be worth this?

Fame. Money. Power. I almost forgot.

"You're . . . the . . . cu . . ." I had to slap myself on

the back of the head to force it out. ". . . Cute . . . One."

"Okay. Maybe I'll cooperate."

"And what's my job?" Ling asked anxiously.

Oh, this was nice. Now I was going to have them all lining up to have the boss lick their boots.

I think not.

"You're the *Lunatic* One," I said, hoping to douse his fire.

"Cool," he said.

All right. This is what I had to work with. I better wind up with a Grammy out of this.

"And speaking of love monkeys," said Steven, "you were doing a pretty mean Tom Jones up there, Wolfgang."

I very deliberately slicked my hair back, and looked off into the distance rather than at my accuser. "Hey, that's my shtick," I said coolly.

Scratch sat on the hood of the car, shaking his head sadly as he plucked away at nothing on his guitar. He was looking extra rough these days, old Scratch. He still had on the same shiny pants, the same no shirt, still needed the same shower he was refusing to take. You could bend his hair into animal shapes, like pipe cleaners. Hey, maybe we could use that. . . .

But somehow he had managed to get even skinnier since he'd been with us. He must have been losing bone or something, because there was just no fat on him anywhere. He never smiled, and his hand-inked tattoos were fading and smudging, making him look a little more past his expiration date every day.

"What's the matter, Scratch?" I asked. "We are perched here on the very brink of megastardom, and you're the second-biggest reason for that, next to myself. You should be feeling pretty satisfied right about now."

He shook his head more, slower, and in broader left-right swings. "This isn't what I do," he said. "I don't understand any of this."

"You don't have to understand it," I assured him. "I'm the manager, remember? All you have to do is go on with your sulking genius noisemaker routine, and I'll handle the rest."

He continued to shake his head. "Before, I thought, Okay, they can play around me if they want, it doesn't make any difference to me. To be honest, I don't even hear any of the rest of you while I'm playing."

That explains a lot.

"But all this, this showtime stuff . . . this ain't what I do at all."

"Shhh," I said, sensing a bad turn in our little chat. "Don't think about what you do, Scratch, just do it."

Everybody went off with his own assignment. Scratch had to stop thinking. Cecil had to start thinking. Jerome had to turn up the wattage on his new He-He-He-Man image so that it would beam out over the video. And the rest of them had to more or less flail their instruments, back me up, and stay out of the spotlights.

"And bring along some girls, if you can."

Thought I might slip that one through as I shoved them out the door. No go.

"Some *what*?" Steven, Jerome, and Ling—the charter guys—hollered together.

"That's the best harmony you guys have mustered the whole time—"

"Wolfgang," Jerome insisted. "If we stand for one thing in this club—"

"Ya, well, we don't," I said. "Think about it. If you really want to make a statement, people have to be listening. And it's a statistically proven fact that nobody listens to a video that doesn't have girls all over the place. And let's face cruel facts here—unless we get a cooler rep, this club hating women is kind of like quitting the football team after you've already been cut."

The three of them stopped arguing with me. They pondered, they huddled. If I didn't have them thinking my way, I at least had them momentarily stunned.

"Are we going to be a football team too?" Cecil asked.

"Could you go get your hammer and finish building us some platforms, Killer? There ya go, run over there, bang some nails."

"Here's the deal," Steven said, speaking for the group. "You can bring girls in here just for the video. Then they have to get out."

"Fair enough."

"But no Nessy," Jerome insisted.

"And absolutely, positively, *no Monica*," Steven said.

"That's a deal," I assured them, raising my hand in that stupid little three-fingered Boy Scout salute.

Now, where could I find Monica again? Oh yes, the ice-cream parlor.

12
So I Ain't No Boy Scout

"Thanks for coming. I'm glad you agreed to meet me."

"I was happy to. It all seems so mysterious and exciting."

"That's me all over, babe. Mysterious and exciting."

I wasn't even exaggerating. Because while I am *always* exciting, this day I was also a man of big mystery. I had called Monica and arranged this secret meeting, probably setting myself up for court-martial. I showed up incognito, wearing a dorky Red Sox baseball cap and windbreaker. I had also penciled in my mustache—not that it needed that much help—and wore small round tortoiseshell glasses that tinted darker when the light hit them. Doof City, so no one would suspect it was me in a million years, even with the wheel-chair.

And we met in the back of the church, just like real mobsters.

"So I suppose you're wondering why we're here," I whispered. There was nobody else in the place, but I think it's impossible to raise your voice in a church unless you're the featured speaker.

"Are we getting married?"

Bolts of lightning *zinging* around in my chest.

"Don't toy with me, you," I said. "I'll have that priest out of the bar and over here in a second."

"You're always so funny," she said, giggling to prove it.

"So how come I'm not your favorite?"

Monica paused, because she is, basically, a kind person. As kind as a female person can manage, anyway.

"Some people might say you're a little . . . scary," she said.

If she thought she was discouraging me, she was quite mistaken.

"Oh they might, might they?"

"Okay, they do."

"There, that's better," I said.

Monica shook her head at me, laughing. "A lot of people might be offended by what I just said. Not you, though. You look like I just handed you money."

"Oh please," I said, wheeling myself away from her. "Don't. That would just embarrass me. Girls are always trying to give me money."

Already, Monica had broken the world church laughter record. "Is it okay to have fun in the church like this?" she asked extra softly.

"I don't know," I answered even more softly. "I think you better come into the confessional booth with me so we can investigate."

"Thanks anyway," she said. "But I don't think I'll be investigating anything with you."

I laughed, because I always laugh at such things. Because that's who Wolf is. But we both knew she meant it, now and forever, and what I wanted to do was *not* laugh.

"Anyway," I said, steering back around to shore, "I don't scare you at all, do I?"

"Nope," she said cheerily. Which made things mostly all better again.

"Okay, so here's the deal," I said, jumping right into manager mode. "We have pulled together the most fantasmic band you ever heard in your whole girly life. We have a guitar player who's like from another planet, and a huge, huge rhythm section that's practically like a whole symphony orchestra. We could knock buildings down, if we wanted to.

And we might want to at some point."

"How cool," Monica said, coolly. Mostly she was being polite, waiting to get to the real point. "Is Steven in the band?"

"See now, here we were having a perfectly nice time, and you had to go and ruin it."

"So that's a yes."

I scowled, to make her wilt. She did not.

"Well, *I'm* the singer, did you know that?"

"When's the show? Where? Will he be expecting me?"

"Wait a minute, wait a minute. What do you think, these tickets are *free*? This is going to be one of those must-see shows that you'll have to be the tenth caller to the radio station to get into. I can't just give—"

"Save it, Wolf. You didn't come to try and squeeze a few cents out of me. What do you think you're do-ing here, *scalping* tickets to a show probably nobody's going to want to see anyway? Get a grip, Oil Slick."

This must be the source of my powerful attraction to Monica: her uncanny resemblance to myself.

And I don't like it one bit.

"Hey now, is honesty really necessary here? I thought you and I were above that."

"Yes, let's be honest. What this is all about is,

you have something I want—Steven. And I have something you want, which is . . . ?"

"All right—girls. Satisfied? A band has to have girls around, it's an unwritten law and everybody knows it. It is more important for a musical group to have girls than to have musical instruments. And somebody's going to film us. If they film us the way we usually look, we'll make the Gregorian Chant guys seem like party animals. You've seen music videos—*dripping* with women."

I had her laughing again, only this time it didn't feel so much like it was something we were sharing. "And you know . . . how many girls personally, Wolfgang?"

"That's kind of an unfair question, don't you think? I mean, who can really even define *know*."

"Hey, I'd be impressed to find that anyone in your club can define *girl*."

"Ouch."

"So what would you say, Wolf? Personally, what do you guess, you might actually be able to round up two, maybe three girls who would talk to you?"

"That's a conservative estimate."

"Okay, and combining that with the girls the rest of the He-Men could bring in would raise the total to . . . ?"

"Two, maybe three," I said quietly. I felt like I was a fighter, flat on the mat, but the referee wouldn't stop counting me out (ninety-nine, one hundred, one hundred and one . . .).

"Which would seem to make me and my friends pretty valuable to you. So I think the real question is, how much are you going to pay *us* per ticket?"

My god, what happened here? She may well be just as wicked as they say she is. She's like me. She's worse than me even. She's—

A goddess.

"We'll have to see how much we can dig up," I said, wheeling myself backward toward the door before she could damage me any further. This was embarrassing. "Just be at the club Saturday, noon. It's going to be colossal."

She was shaking her head as I pushed open the big wooden door, bringing down a shaft of white light on her frizzy red head. "Who'd ever have thought it, you guys coming around to us like this?"

"Hey," I said, "we're just like any rock-and-roll outfit—just 'cause we hate women doesn't mean we don't love 'em."

I shoved myself out the door before she could top me.

13
Sniff This

I had to be quiet. After all, Lars worked there, and Scratch lived there. Not that they should mind, since we all knew who had really become the star of the show.

"Killer, you do beautiful work, honest. I'm tempted to travel all the way down to Muscle Shoals, Alabama, just to visit that silo you and your uncle built. I bet it's like some kind of shrine, with pilgrims coming from all over to see it."

Cecil allowed himself a moment of pride, something we didn't see too much of with him. "Well, we have had 'em from as far as Huntsville and Biloxi."

"Wow!" I exclaimed, maybe with a little too much gusto. "Huntsville and Biloxi. That's remarkable. Say, while we're jawing here, how 'bout you take *my* platform, ya, that nice one there with the great little ramp, and kind of just haul it right over . . . come on, there you go . . . a little farther, now center it. Perfect!"

"But you're so far away from everybody else's platform, and stuck in this greasy ol' bay. What if Lars has to put up a car? No, I'll just find you a better spot and—"

"Leave it right where it is, Goober," I snapped. "And here, over in the corner, this is where I want you sitting. During the performance, when I give you the signal, I want you to pull that lever right there."

"What's that gonna—"

"Just pull it, pull it, pull the lever, pull the lever!"

This is what is known as the strain of command.

"Is there a problem?" Scratch asked, crawling out of his bed in the car, stretching, and strapping on his guitar the way the rest of us pull on socks at the beginning of the day.

"Good," I said. "You'll be there." I pointed out one of two small platforms off to the right, out of my spotlight. Scratch yawned, shrugged, and went over to sit on it. "Anyone got a pen?" he asked.

Lars clomped onto the scene, wearing his own guitar. He pulled a pen from behind his ear and took his place next to Scratch without having to be told. I had to say this for Lars, he made a great guitar sidekick. If only we could get him to sound a little less musical.

Jerome came in wearing a baseball hat and a long rubber raincoat, eyes darting, checking every corner of the building for danger.

"She's not here, is she?"

"Ness the Mess?" I asked.

He shuddered.

"Nah, you're safe." I pointed him to his box.

"Don't you have something a little more toward the back?" he asked.

"Sorry, that's where drummers go. Don't worry, Studley, you'll be fine. Just don't throw off any clothes or anything."

Jerome's face turned so red from the mere suggestion that I think we could feel safe that he would not be disrobing for the camera.

Steven came in, wearing a button-down shirt, a button-down face, and a buttoned-up lip. Silently, he mounted the small stage where his stuff had been set up. He picked up his sticks and stared out into space.

The tension coming from Steve-o was giving off sparks. I wheeled right up to him.

"Stage fright?" I asked, in an honest attempt to be helpful.

"Take a walk," he growled.

Get it? Take a walk? Wheelchair? A most wicked thing to say.

Times like these bring Steve-o and me close.

"Listen," I said. "I know you threw up on TV that one other time, but this is different. You won't have to answer anybody's questions. The crowd is not going to be against us. . . ."

"And Monica's not gonna be here, right, Wolfgang?" he blurted.

I thought that was a little strong.

"Steven. I'm hurt that you'd even ask me. Did I not agree not to bring her?"

"You slug," he said. "If she shows up, I'm going to beat you to death with my own two drumsticks."

I gave him a big fake yawn. "Fine, as long as you don't lose the beat. You are a professional, remember." Then I reached up—he didn't even lean closer when he saw me straining—and unbuttoned the top four buttons of his shirt. He stared at me as if I'd taken food off his plate. "There's an extra two bucks in it for you," I said. "You've got thirty-nine chest hairs, Steven. Use 'em."

We were all in place when Sammy Blue and his crew of one came in. Sammy carried a large, fancy reel-to-reel recorder with him, and his assistant carried a big videocam-lighting setup.

"By the way," Steven asked, "what song do they want to record?"

"Sammy said we can do whatever we want. So I decided to unveil our first single, 'Sniff This.' "

Groans went up from each little platform, except Scratch's.

"Wolf, what is 'Sniff This'?" Jerome asked. "How are we going to play a song we have not rehearsed, and we have never heard before? What are we going to play?"

"You're going to play the same thing you always play. Jerome, who do you think you're talking to here? I know what we do, remember? Every song is the same. You guys just whack away back there and I'll sing. When the words change, it's a new song."

Jerome relaxed. "Oh ya, I forgot."

"Okay now, people, let's not get caught up in our own myth, shall we?"

Again, a rhetorical question. Again, Cecil.

"Okay, we won't."

The equipment was set up, the one big light crisping us like french fries, when His Lingness finally arrived. Even I was impressed.

He wore lemon-colored pants made out of parachute material. He wore the shiniest forest-green sport coat I had ever seen, with the seams all visible, and with no shirt underneath. He wore an oversize mariachi band hat and the tiniest granny sunglasses that made his face look the size of Greenland. And he had somebody with him.

"Nice jacket, Ling," I said as I stared past him at his guest.

"I know," he answered. "It's the lining. It's the nuttiest thing, you know. With the coolest part of the jacket hidden on the inside, why doesn't everybody wear them this way?"

"Ya," I murmured. "Nutty. Who's your friend, Ling?"

"She's not my friend, she's my mother."

I grabbed him by the arm and yanked him down close for a good He-Man scolding. "You brought your *mom*?"

"You said to bring girls. She's the only girl I know. Anyway, she's psyched—she'll make a great audience."

"Ya, but . . ." I tried to be delicate, which we know is not my regular mode. "But she looks like *you*"—which she most certainly did. I think they even shared clothes.

Ling looked at his mother. She smiled at him. He smiled at her. He turned back to me. "Ya, so what's your point?"

Even I could not be that mean. At least we could finally break the secret of Ling-Ling's real name.

"Have a seat, Mrs. . . . ?"

"Ling," she said.

"Of course," I sighed.

I made sure the technician shined the light right in Steven's eyes when the fans poured in. But I knew it was just a stall tactic. I think he smelled her.

"I'm going to kill you, Wolfgang," he hissed from behind me.

"You'll thank me when you're famous," I said.

"I'm going to be famous for killing you," he answered.

We had just enough girls, and a few degenerate, rock-and-roll-looking bony boys, to be totally legit when taping started.

"All right," Sammy called, clapping his hands. "We'll do this in two stages. First will be strictly audio. I want you to do one take of the song first, then we'll do the videotape second. Got it?"

We got it. It was like the rodeo bull that's caged up until the last second before he comes blasting out of the gate trying to kick the stupid cowboy off his back and into the next world. Sammy hadn't gotten the words out before Scratch tore into his guitar, Steven mauled his drums, and the rest of them kicked in behind.

The fans went right into high-pitch screech.

"Trade with me!" Jerome screamed at Ling when Nessy made her first lunge at his ankle. Jerome had to kick her off.

Ling was only too happy to move up front, and the switch went off in mid-performance without a hitch. Jerome breathed a little easier and beat holy hamburger out of his tambourine, and Ling slapped the bass drum deliriously with his forehead.

"Johnny!!!!!" came Monica's lovely, squealy voice. "Oh Johnnyyyyyy! Beat that drum, you big, strong savage."

How could you not love that woman? What a shame she was wasted on Steve-o He-Mannequin.

Because we had not rehearsed the song—had not rehearsed anything, actually—we sounded our absolute best. The band was motoring along on all cylinders when I finally kicked in. I closed my eyes and forgot all about Barry Manilow and Neil Diamond and the Vienna Boys Choir singing the

Beatles and all that other stuff they nearly broke me with in therapy. I made two rock-hard fists, punched myself once in the temple and once in the solar plexus, and I sang.

All right, I didn't sing. I screamed, equal parts gangsta rap, heavy metal squall, and a Reverend Jesse Jackson preach speech.

> *We don't like girls*
> *But we don't like boys*
> *And we don't know what we're sayin'*
> *But we make a lot of noise*
> *And we can't play music*
> *But we can't play football*
> *But we must know somethin'*
> *'Cause we're takin' dough from you-all*
>
> *SNIFF THIS!*
> *I say we're takin' dough from you-all*
> *SNIFF THIS!*
> *Ya, we're takin' dough from you-all.*

I paused to take note, and Sammy was ecstatic. He was making that foolish little A-okay sign with his fingers, and shouting, "More, more, more," at us along with the assembled adoring fandom. I think I'll have "More, more, more" on my head-stone, the way people keep yelling it at me.

If, that is, I ever decide to die.

> And all the girlies love Chesthair
> And Jerome, the King of Ting
> But they know they're gettin' nowhere
> 'Cause we're He-Men and we sing

> SNIFF THIS!
> Yes we're the He-Men and we sing
> SNIFF THIS!
> If you don't like it talk to Ling.

Now, by the third time around, the crowd had caught Sniff fever, and I held out the microphone for them to deliver the SNIFF THIS! line. By the fifth round, the Sniffs themselves had figured it out, musically challenged though they were.

> So one of us vomits
> And one of us cries
> And one of us eats car parts
> And one of us lies
> We ain't losin' sleep
> And you can't make us think

110

We ain't changin' nothin'
You love us 'cause we stink.
So Sir Scratch won't change his clothes
And we couldn't whip the Girl Scouts
But you know you're gonna join in
When the Wolf-man tells ya shout out

SNIFF THIS!
Let's go scratchin' and a-sniffin'
SNIFF THIS!
While we're wailin' and a-riffin'
SNIFF THIS!
Can you guess what we been rollin' in?
SNIFF THIS!
It's the shorts your dad went bowlin' in. . . .

We didn't want to stop. They made us. It was time to do the video portion of the program. Right away while we were still sweaty. The crowd was frenzied. Monica and her gang of savage Girl Scouts—in full uniform, of course—were throwing shoes and oil cans and whatever they could find on the garage floor. Loch Nessy was trying desperately to get at our poor Jerome while being restrained by Mrs. Ling, who I'm sure was convinced the girl was after her teen idol son.

All Sammy Blue could do was pace back and forth while his cameraman prepared, muttering loudly to himself, "I'm gonna win, I'm gonna win, I know I'm gonna win this time."

Huh?

No matter. We were on cloud He-Man. All we could manage to do, communication-wise, was high-five and slap each other and throw things at each other and make animal noises.

Like zoo gorillas.

Like guys. Guy communication.

Except Scratch. Scratch just turned off his volume and kept on playing.

"We're ready now!" Sammy exclaimed. We all fell silent to listen to instructions. "This time, all I want you to do is fake it."

As club leader, I spoke up for the band.

"Huh?"

"You know, I'm going to play the tape back for you to hear, but I'm not going to be recording any sound. I'll use the separate sound recording. For the video, you just go through the motions."

Pause ten seconds for it to sink in, then I wheeled around to face my troops.

"Lip-synch!" I screamed, and the whole high-five, gorilla celebration started again. "Now we *know* we've made big time, if they want us to lip-synch a video!"

Eventually, we calmed down enough for them to start the audio. It took a few seconds to get used to it. Then we kicked in and started the faking.

Steven looked nervous all over again. It's a video thing.

Lars looked just as wooden and artificial as always.

Cecil looked like he was unaware that we were not, actually, playing the song. There was some kind of genius in there somewhere.

Jerome stared into the camera like one of those kidnap victims being forced at gunpoint to say everything was swell.

Scratch kept shaking his head, but what are you going to do?

Thank god we had me and Ling. Freed from the burden of actually playing, Ling did his tricks, twirling his sticks like batons. Tossing them up in the air like he was juggling torches. Blowing kisses to his mother. Ling had a definite future as a professional faker.

But I did it because I am simply a pro. I held the microphone close, I played to it. The microphone loved me. I played to the camera. No surprise, the camera also loved me. I rolled down my custom-made ramp, and played to the audience. You can guess the result.

At one point the camera swung around to pan our intimate but enthusiastic gathering. Monica and her gang unfurled a bedsheet with GIRL SCOUTS HAVE CHESTHAIR FEVER printed in brilliant red block letters.

This was my moment. We rounded into the home stretch, final chorus. I waved the signal to my man Cecil. My man Cecil missed the signal. I waved it again, taking advantage of the nonaudio recording to shout *Cecil!*

He got the message. I wheeled myself back up onto the platform, Cecil pulled the lever and . . . I was up, on Lars's awesome hydraulic lift. Microphone in hand, I smiled, looked *down* on the rest of the band, looked *down* on the audience, looked *down* into the camera, which looked back up at me like a baby bird to its mother.

Portrait of a rock star. This was it, the absolute zenith of life. Me on my platform six feet above the rest of the screaming, teeming world.

By the time the song wound down and Cecil lowered me, I could already see myself in one of those paperback biographies in the rack at CVS, telling how I got where I am today. The other guys were in there too, but mostly it was about me.

"I could not have imagined it any better," Sammy was gushing as he rushed up to us. "This is going to be absolutely unbeatable. All you guys need to do now is sign these releases." He quickly stuck these sheets in each band member's hands.

You could almost hear a group gasp.

"Excuse me, Mr. Blue," I said as calmly as I could.

The top line of the release form read *America's Funniest Home Videos.*

"You want to tell me what this is about?"

"Oh ya," he said, still breathless with excitement. "I have been trying *so* long to get on this program, you have no idea. I tried the animal tricks video, the dangerous-stunts-that-end-in-disaster type video, the calling-up-people-and-telling-them-relatives-were-dead prank video . . . but this, this is it. You guys are going to *kill* them. I took this smoothie singer I found at a wedding, and I'm dubbing your audio over his video and his audio over your—"

Claannggg!

It was the sweetest music we ever made. It was the sound of Scratch's guitar hitting the video camera.

Clangggg!

That was the reel-to-reel.

"I'm going to sue!" Sammy screamed. "Do you know how much money—"

Sammy ran toward Scratch, who raised the guitar high once more. Sammy stopped, with his flunky right behind. The crowd was almost all gone now, the last few emptying out the back of the garage quickly, as agreed. No one noticed. The show was over.

"Get the audio tape," Scratch said to Ling. "Jerome, you get the video."

"You are going to jail, kid," Sammy said.

"No way," Scratch said. "Those tapes belong to Scratch and the Sniffs."

We collected our tapes, they collected their equipment, and we split up.

"At least we can add this to our one-of-a-kind tape collection," Jerome joked.

Nobody said another word about it.

Not even me.

We knew we had a new boss man. There was no debate, no discussion. I wouldn't fight it, and even Steven agreed. We didn't even bother taking an official vote.

Those of us who actually lived off-site came into the club together that morning, with an unusual singularity of purpose. We went, as a team, right up to the Lincoln. Steven opened the door of the car to wake Scratch and give him the news.

But he wasn't there. His little bag of belongings, his guitar, his person, were gone.

"Well, he got a good healthy start to his journey," Steven said, pulling himself back out of the car. "He ate the gearshift knob."

I sniffed at the car. At least he'd left his scent behind.